payback

"[In *Bad Connection,*] Carlson handles the controversial gift of visions with great integrity and care. Scriptures are strategically sprinkled throughout the book in such a way they not only let readers know what's in the Bible, but add to the story as well."

the secret life of Samantha McGregor
BOOK FOUR

payback

a novel

---

melody carlson

MULTNOMAH
BOOKS

PAYBACK

Scripture quotations are taken from the King James Version.

The characters and events in this book are fictional, and any resemblance to actual persons or events is coincidental.

Trade Paperback ISBN 978-1-59052-934-8
eBook ISBN 978-0-307-56153-4

Published in the United States by Multnomah, an imprint of the Crown Publishing Group, a division of Penguin Random House LLC, New York.

MULTNOMAH® and its mountain colophon are registered trademarks of Penguin Random House LLC.

Printed in the United States of America

Author's Note

I normally don't include a letter in my books, but because The Secret Life of Samantha McGregor series treads on some new territory, I want to make a few things as clear as possible.

First of all, this book is *fiction*—it's simply a story that's meant to entertain and to possibly point out some spiritual truths—but it is *not* a theological study on the proper use of the gifts of the Holy Spirit. While I do believe in the gifts of the Holy Spirit and in God's desire for all of us to do many wonderful things, I also realize that Samantha's gift, her ability to receive dreams and visions from God, is extremely rare. But it does make for a good story!

Second, my hope is that you won't envy Samantha's unusual gift or seek it for yourself, since that would be totally wrong! Don't forget that God is the giver of every good and perfect gift, and *He's* the One who decides who gets what and when it's appropriate to use. If you go around searching for your own gifts, you can put yourself at serious risk. Satan masquerades as an angel of light and delights in tricking those who look for gifts in the wrong places. Don't let that be you.

More than anything, I hope you'll follow Samantha's example by seeking out God and a committed relationship with Him. I hope you'll desire to walk closely with God every day, to make Him your best friend, and to be ready for whatever adventures and gifts He has in store for you. Just make sure they come from God.

And finally, remember that the Bible is our ultimate source for answers to all of life's questions. Also, please check out the resources and discussion questions in the back of this book.

I pray that this fictional journey will draw your heart closer to God and that He will be your lifeline—for today and for always!

Best blessings,

Melody Carlson

A Word from Samantha

The first time it happened, I thought it was pretty weird but kind of cool. The second time it happened, I got a little freaked. The third time it happened, I became seriously scared and had sort of a meltdown. That's when my mom decided to send me to a shrink. She thought I was going crazy. And I thought she was right for a change.

Turns out it was just God. Okay, not just God. Because, believe me, God is way more than just anything. Still, it was hard to explain this weird phenomenon to my mom or the shrink or anyone. It still is. Other than my best friend, Olivia, I don't think most people really get me.

But that's okay, because I know that God gets me. For that reason I try to keep this part of my life under wraps. For the most part anyway.

A Word from the Word...

And ye shall know that I am in the midst of Israel, and that I am the LORD your God, and none else: and my people shall never be ashamed. And it shall come to pass afterward, that I will pour out my spirit upon all flesh; and your sons and your daughters shall prophesy, your old men shall dream dreams, your young men shall see visions: And also upon the servants and upon the handmaids in those days will I pour out my spirit. (Joel 2:27–29, KJV)

With arms spread wide, the blonde steps back, staring down at her mint green formal gown now splattered with spots of bright red blood. When she looks up, her eyes widen in horror. She sees her date, a dark-haired young man in a neat black tux, his face twisted in pain as his fists tighten and he crumples to the floor. He curls into a prenatal ball…and a bright, shiny pool of blood stains the clean white floor around him. Music blares in the background, the bass thumping a fast beat. It's a Pretty Ricky song, but the only sound the pretty blonde hears is coming from her boyfriend as he lets out a low growl followed by a gurgle. Then he jerks suddenly, convulsing, drawing a final gasping breath.

The girl bends down, reaches out her hand as if she wants to help him, and then as if sensing danger or perhaps seeing someone now threatening her, she stands and backs away with a horrified look, turns, and desperately dashes in the opposite direction, tripping over her spiky high heels but continuing on…as if she is running for her life.

But it's too late. More shots ring out in fast repetition and more screams of terror. All I can see is red now—blood is everywhere.

It's a massacre.

I wake up clinging to my comforter and still shaking. My heart pounds with a very real sense of fear, as if I, too, am in grave danger. It takes a long moment to realize that this was only a dream. Just a dream. But a realistic and horribly tragic dream. Without turning on the bedside lamp, I reach for the notebook I keep handy for times like this, and in the gray dawn light, I take several deep, calming breaths and begin to write.

I'm trying to capture all the still-vivid details, the style of the mint green gown (beaded with spaghetti straps, formfitting—the girl had a good figure) and those metallic-toned shoes (were they bronze or gold?). I try to recall the girl's facial features (what made her so pretty?). I do remember what appeared to be diamond earrings, three piercings in one ear, smallest on top, largest on the bottom. But was it only one ear? And if so, which ear was it? Right or left? I close my eyes and try to see her again. Left. I believe it was left.

I remember the boy's hairstyle, short and neat, as if he might be into athletics. I try to describe his tux, but other than black, I draw a blank. I can't even remember his shoes, but I think they were black as well. I write down a description of the floor as I remember it—large square tiles of white with streaks of gray throughout. Marble perhaps? I describe what the music sounded like. (I don't even know why I think it was a Pretty Ricky song since I'm not a fan, but it's what went through my head.) And then I remember strings of lights glowing blurrily in the background. Like a party going on. A wedding perhaps?

I pause, searching my memory for more, trying to figure out if I've missed an important detail. Another person? A sound? A smell? Who had the gun? Or was the guy even killed with a gun? Perhaps it was a knife. I don't remember that part at all. Did I even see what happened? Is it possible that the girl was responsible? No, she seemed too shocked, too frightened. And yet if she'd committed a crime, perhaps in the heat of the moment, it would make sense that she'd be shocked and scared. I make note of this too. But there must have been more. Was there some little detail I missed? Did I forget something? I shut my eyes again and just sit there in bed, trying to remember. But that seems to be it.

I close my notebook and set it back on the bedside table. I will tell Ebony about this dream later today. I lie back down, breathing deeply to calm myself, but who can sleep after a dream like that? I wish I could call Olivia and run it past her. I'm sure she'd have some thoughts. But it's not even six yet. Instead, I go to the kitchen and try to be quiet as I make coffee.

It must've been a prom, I decide as I pour water into the coffee maker. And that makes sense because it's spring, and already people are starting to pair off and plan for prom at my school. Even Olivia is beginning to talk about it. She's pretty sure Alex is going to ask her. Naturally, she thinks Conrad will ask me. And I think it'd be fun to go to prom. It'd be a first for me, for sure. But what if there's going to be a murder that night? Still, I didn't recognize either of the people in my dream. And the girl, especially, had the kind of looks that a person would remember. She looked the type who would be well known. But I've never seen her before. I am certain of that. Still, I suppose she could be new at school…or possibly she hasn't started going there yet. Maybe today will be her first day. The guy was unfamiliar too. I didn't get a very good look at his face. But for some reason, he struck me as athletic. That might've just been the hair. Although it seems he was tall, well built. I better make a note of that.

Our prom is still a month away, so that gives me time. Unless it's not our prom. What if it's another school's prom? Who knows what dates that might include? I know schools like to stagger the dates so all the local restaurants aren't overwhelmed with high school students going out to dinner before their proms. It's possible another high school could have a prom as soon as next weekend. I will have to mention this to Ebony ASAP.

I pour a cup of coffee, add some milk, and go into the living room and sit by the window to watch as the morning slowly comes. I think about Zach now. And as I often do in the morning, I pray for him. He's back in rehab again. The good thing is that he actually wanted to go this time. Even though it was not optional, he was happy to go. He knew that he needed it, that he was lucky to get this second chance. And he promised Mom and me that things are really going to be different when he comes back this time. But that won't be for six months. Still, he didn't complain. I know he was thinking it was better than doing prison time. And that was a very real possibility. If Zach hadn't fully cooperated with the DA and police like he did, I'm sure he would be in prison right now. As it was, he spent several weeks in jail. That in itself was sobering—in more than one way. And although I'm still sad—for Zach's sake—I am so thankful he is alive. Things could've gone so differently. I'm thankful for something else too. Zach is finally returning to God. He told me that right before he left for rehab. He asked me to look for his old Bible and send it to him. I promised to send him a Bible, whether or not I found his old one. But I did find his, and I sent it just last week.

"You're up early," Mom says as she comes down the stairs still wearing her bathrobe.

"Yeah…" I consider telling her about my dream, but it still bothers her that I get these dreams and visions. Despite making some baby steps of progress, she has a long way to go before she completely accepts my unusual gift. I figure it will come when she returns fully to God. In the meantime, I need to be patient and careful not to overload her. And I need to pray.

Mom gets her coffee and comes into the living room to join me. "Spring really seems to be here," she says, looking out the window. "Are you making any plans for summer yet?"

I shrug. "Not really. I mean, sure, I'd love to head to Europe with some girlfriends and have a good time, but I don't think it's likely." I laugh and try not to feel envious that my best friend might be doing just that this summer.

"No, not likely. But I really wish I could give you those things, Sam. I would if I could. But as usual, finances are tight." She sighs sadly.

"I don't expect those things," I say quickly. "In fact, the truth is I don't think I'm ready for Europe yet. I'll probably be better off sticking around here. I've heard stories about kids my age getting into serious trouble over there."

She sort of laughs. "You're not one of *those* kinds of kids, Samantha. You have a level head. I would trust you to go any-where and not get in trouble."

"Thanks, Mom. But if that's true, you have God to thank."

She nods and takes a sip of coffee.

I can tell my not-so-subtle hint hasn't hit pay dirt.

"I better get ready for work. Thanks for making coffee."

"No problem."

She pauses at the foot of the stairs. "By the way, I'm going out with Steven tonight…might be late."

"Don't do anything I wouldn't do," I tease her.

She makes a face. "How about you? Any plans?"

"Olivia wanted to go to a movie. I'm guessing Alex and Conrad will join us."

Mom smiles now. "That's nice."

I want to ask her why she thinks that's nice. Is it because it alleviates her guilt for spending so much time with Steven lately? Or is it because that makes me seem like a more "normal" girl and that makes her feel relieved? Or is it something else? Those questions could sound as if I'm inviting a fight. And I'm not. I'm just curious.

I'm used to the fact that Mom and I still lead fairly separate lives. I know this is partly due to the demands of her job and of being a single parent. And I can't help but wonder how different life would be if Dad were still alive. I'm sure everything would be much better if he hadn't been killed. But I suppose I could be wrong. As unlikely as it seems, it's possible that things might've gone in an even worse direction for our family. For instance, what if my parents were divorced, like so many of my friends' parents, and I were torn between the two of them? Even so, I'd still be glad to have my dad around.

Maybe it's better to simply not consider those what-if scenarios. Besides, I need to trust God with the big, impossible-to-understand situations. And He is worthy of my trust. He's proven this to me time and again.

Still, as I go upstairs to get ready for school, I feel a flicker of resentment about my lonely family life. I mean, it's not like we can do anything about Zach being gone. Or Dad for that matter. But not long ago, I had hoped that Mom and I were starting to get closer. We'd just begun doing more things together. We were even talking more. And Mom was trying to work less. Then just as it seemed that my relationship with her was really changing, Steven Lowery stepped into the picture. As a result, I feel slightly pushed aside.

Okay, I know it seems incredibly selfish, not to mention juvenile, to be jealous of Mom's boyfriend. And it's hard to admit this, even if only to myself, but I still do resent him…just a little. Yet at the same time, I'm glad for Mom. The truth is, Steven really seems to make her happy. In some ways she seems happier than she's been in years. I'm sure it's wrong for me to have these negative feelings toward him. I mean, he's always doing things for her. He buys her things and takes her places. He compliments her on her appearance. And even though she's ten years older than he is, I know he makes her feel beautiful. She actually told me this just a few days ago.

Seriously, I scold myself as I get into the shower, *I am a selfish, selfish daughter.* I should just grow up. I should be thankful for Steven being in the picture. And I should be happy for Mom. And I should be praying for both of them. After all, it was only last night that Mom said, "Steven is so good…so good for me… He's almost too good to be real."

Okay, maybe that's what bothers me. It could be one of the consequences of working for the police department and solving some pretty hideous crimes—perhaps I've gotten a little jaded at the ripe old age of seventeen—but I do believe that when something seems too good to be real, it usually isn't real.

t sounds like a prom," says Olivia on the way to school. I'm driving today. We take turns now that I have my cool little green VW Bug.

"I know," I agree. "I thought maybe a wedding, but this time of year, it really could be a prom."

"Do you think it's ours?"

So I describe the girl to her, including the three diamond earrings in her left ear. "But I didn't recognize her."

"I'm sure there are kids in school that you wouldn't recognize, Sam. Brighton is pretty big."

"Yeah, but this seemed like the kind of girl you'd notice. Like a fairly popular girl, kind of an A-list girl, you know."

"Oh…"

"And my best guess was that the guy was kind of a jock."

"Like king and queen of the prom?"

"Sort of like that."

"But he was dead?"

"Yeah."

"Creepy."

"I know." I try not to think too much about this image as I drive. It really is creepy. I've had dreams of other serious things, including deaths, but something about the blood-splattered formal and the look on that girl's face just feels more extreme than usual.

"Have you called Detective Hamilton yet?"

"No, Ebony doesn't usually get to the station until nine. I'll call her after first period."

"What a gorgeous day," Olivia says as I stop for the traffic light. "You should open the sunroof, Sam."

"Good idea." So I reach up and slide it open. "Woo-hoo!" I shout as I wave my hand in the relatively warm morning air.

"TGIF!" shouts Olivia as she sticks out her hand too.

"It feels almost like summer," I say as the light turns green.

"Do you realize there's less than two months of school left?"

"Yeah…my mom was just asking me what I plan to do for summer vacation."

"I told my mom that I wanted to go to Europe last night, and she said no way unless she went with me."

"That would be okay, wouldn't it?" Once again I try not to feel envious of my best friend. I actually think it's very cool that Olivia's mom likes doing things with her daughter. I guess I just wish my mom could be more like that. Even with Steven in the picture, I wish she wanted to take time away from him so she and I could do more things together. But there I go being selfish again.

"I guess…" Olivia sighs loudly. "But going to Europe with your mom seems a little lame."

"Better than not going at all."

"I suppose. And if Mom goes, at least we'll stay in nice places, eat good meals, and do some great shopping."

"That sounds way too fun."

"Why don't you come too, Sam?"

"I wish…"

"Why not?"

"Well, for one thing I can't afford it. But also I'm secretly hoping I can work with the police a little more this summer."

"Have they asked you?"

"No…but it would sure beat working at the day care again. Not that I don't like those little rug rats, but doing police work is way more interesting, and now that Ebony has given me some special training and I have this car, well, it'd be fun to put it all to better use."

I pull into the school parking lot, and as we get out of the car, I notice a blond girl who reminds me of the one in my dream. "Hey, look. Do you know who that is?"

Olivia peers at the girl getting out of a small white car. "Yeah, that's Laura Temple. She's in my chem class."

"By any chance does she have three piercings in her left ear?"

Olivia laughs, then gets a somber expression. "I don't know…but I can check."

We wait as the girl slowly walks toward us, but as she gets closer and I can see her face more clearly, I know she's not the girl from last night's dream. "Never mind," I say to Olivia as we start walking toward the school. "It's not her anyway."

"How can you be so sure?"

"It's just not. The girl in my dream was strikingly pretty. Not that Laura's a dog or anything, but she's just not the same girl, okay?"

"What if she has those same earrings?" teased Olivia.

"Then I'll reconsider."

"Hey, Sam," calls Jack as we walk across the street. He's having what I'm guessing is his last before-school cigarette.

"What's up?" I pause and smile at him. I know that he's still getting over Felicity's death. I think we all are. But in some ways Jack's opened up since all that happened. Or maybe it's just that more people started reaching out to him and he realized he still has friends.

"Not much," he says as he blows out a puff of smoke. "Nice day, huh?"

"Totally," says Olivia. "Will you be at band practice tomorrow?"

"Uh-huh." He nods and takes in a long drag.

"I'll see ya there," Olivia says as we head into the building.

"Catch ya later," I call. "Don't be late for class, Jack." I hear his sarcastic laugh as I go inside, and I can tell he's thinking, *Yeah, sure. Since when do I care?* But I hope he'll start caring. I hope he'll begin to see that his life has more value than just hanging and acting tough. Still, he's made some progress. And he's talking to us. That's worth a lot.

Olivia and I part ways, and as I navigate the crowded halls, I keep my eyes peeled for a pretty blonde with three piercings in one ear. And while I see girls who sort of fit the image, I already know and recognize these girls, and it's obvious that none of them is the one from my dream. More and more I am convinced that my dream is not about our school. And maybe it's not even a prom. It could be a wedding or some other formal occasion.

After Creative Writing, I call Ebony and quickly explain the dream to her. When she asks for more details, I pull out my notebook and read the whole thing to her. "My first guess is that it's a prom," I finally tell her. "But I suppose it could be a wedding or something."

"Okay, let's start with the first possibility. If it's a prom, do you think it's your school? Was it the Brighton High prom?"

"I don't know... The girl and guy were totally unfamiliar."

"When is your prom?"

"The second weekend of May."

"That's almost a month out."

"I know..."

"But if it's not Brighton's prom, it could be sooner."

"Exactly what I was thinking."

"Well, this is helpful for starters," she says. "How about I do some initial research on who's having proms and where and when and you come by after school so we can kick it around some more? Okay?"

"Sounds good." I hang up and think how much I like working with Ebony. It's ironic that she used to be Dad's partner. But I suppose that's part of the reason she gets me. Also, she seems to understand my gift. And she's a Christian. All in all, I feel really blessed to know her—and to work with her.

"Hey, Sam," says Conrad as he catches me on my way to Journalism. "What's up?"

"Not much."

"Want to go out tonight?"

"Sure. What did you have in mind?"

"Well, Alex said that Olivia suggested a movie. But not a chick flick, I hope."

"Oh yeah," I tease. "I heard it involves lots of designer clothes and killer shoes, not to mention giggling and chocolate, and I think there's an over-the-top wedding and—"

"Come on, Sam." His pale brows pull together in a slight frown.

I wink at him. "Actually, I think you'll like it."

"Cool." He smiles in relief, then waves as he takes off.

"Later," I call out as I watch him jogging down the breeze-way, trying to beat the bell. His long lanky form topped by that curly red hair looks slightly comical from here. I chuckle to myself, then turn and go into the classroom, where whatever seemed humorous suddenly evaporates.

I still get jolted by the loss of Felicity every time I walk into Journalism. We had this class together, and I'd been trying to get to know her—I'd actually been making progress. There was no denying the girl was definitely a misfit, but she was also interesting and intelligent. Too smart, I'd hoped, to be involved in the kind of crud she'd been involved in. Then, even when I tried to warn her, actually telling her of my vision, she had refused to listen or to take me seriously.

At first I blamed myself for her death…but I'm slowly coming to grips with it. I realize that God uses all sorts of stuff to guide us and to warn us, but it's up to us to pay attention, to heed the signs, and to respond accordingly. Felicity refused to do that. Now she's dead. Still, it's sad. Very, very sad.

Thinking of Felicity makes me even more determined to uncover what last night's dream was about—and who was in danger. I just hope I figure it out in time to prevent another death. I don't think I can bear to see someone else getting hurt. So I shoot up a quick prayer, once again asking God to help me, to guide me…asking that I'll be tuned in to hear Him.

I can't imagine how I would deal with my life without God. These visions and dreams would probably drive me seriously crazy—straight to the loony bin. But knowing that they come from Him and that He has the answers makes all the difference. Consequently, I am able to focus on my classes for the better part of the day. And I nearly forget about those hard-to-understand things like dreams and visions until the school day is almost done.

I'm on my way to my last class, which is Art, when something stops me. Because the art building is separate and a good distance from the Social Studies department, where I've just been, I'm hurrying across a mostly deserted walkway. But as I turn a corner, something catches my attention in the covered walkway ahead. So I slow down to see what it is. But as I look, I experience that familiar flash of light—my clue that what I'm seeing isn't really there. I stand still and continue to watch, focusing as much with my inner vision as with anything else.

At first I think I see a group of five or six guys just messing around. But then I realize the group is picking on a smaller guy. He's your average-looking kid, dressed in ordinary sort of clothes, and he's wearing glasses. He's now being pushed and shoved back and forth, and I briefly wonder if it's my friend and lab partner, Garrett Pierson. But then I get a closer look and realize it's not him. This kid has sandy-colored hair that's sort of wavy. I see a glimpse of his face, and he seems angry at first, but then he becomes seriously frightened as the bullies get rougher with him.

If this was actually happening in real life, I wouldn't hesitate to run over there and yell at those stupid thugs. I'd tell them they were big cowards and bullies, and somehow I'd make them stop. But it's not really happening. At least not right now. Not right here. It's a vision, and as a result I have no control.

I simply stand there and watch as one of the bullies lands his fist right in the victim's face, resulting in a bloody nose. A few more hits, kicks, and punches. Then they all laugh and take off running.

Just like that the whole thing vanishes. Now you see it, now you don't. Even so, the adrenaline is still pumping through me, and my heart is pounding like I've just sprinted a hundred meters. And I feel frustrated and angry, like I just witnessed a crime but could do nothing about it. Hopefully, it hasn't happened yet... Maybe I can do something to prevent it from happening at all.

My hands are still shaky as I walk into the art room, late. Thankfully, Mrs. Morrow seldom marks anyone tardy, and she simply looks up and smiles at me like "no problem." So I go to my favorite table in the back of the room and try to understand what I just witnessed. Although it makes no sense. I try to link it to the dream I had last night, but nothing in this vision seems related to the other. The only common denominator is that I don't know any of the people in the dream or the vision. But that in itself isn't so unusual. For some reason God gives me only a few pieces, and I have to work to fit them together. I guess it's a way for me to partner with Him.

So I attempt to sort the vision out. For starters, the boy being picked on was totally unfamiliar, and although I couldn't see the faces of the bullies clearly, they didn't seem familiar either. Of course, every school, including Brighton, has guys like that. The type who pick on others for no reason except that they can. And I suspect they usually get away with it too. Before I start working on my charcoal sketch, I pull out my notebook and write down exactly what I remember about the vision. It doesn't seem like much, but if God gave me that vision, there must be a reason for it. It's possible that it's connected to the shooting dream I had last night. But the general feeling of the vision, as well as the setting, the people, the time of day, the level of seriousness—it all seems dissimilar. My inclination is that these are two totally separate situations.

After seventh period ends, I walk slowly back toward the main building. I look all around as I stroll along, and I have my cell phone on and ready to make a call. I am seriously hoping to spot the group of thugs, hoping to catch them and to stop them before they have a chance to pounce on the sandy-haired kid with glasses. But I make it all the way back to the locker bay without seeing one single thing that's even slightly out of the ordinary.

"Everything okay?" asks Olivia when I join her at our locker.

"I guess…"

"What's up?" she asks with curiosity.

I quickly explain my latest vision.

"But you didn't know any of the guys?"

"No. I got a look at the kid being bullied, but I couldn't really see the others too well. The guy getting beat up was totally unfamiliar."

"Still, you don't know everyone in this school."

"Obviously not. And I'm sure there could be someone like that around here that I never noticed before."

Just then Olivia nods over to where a short, blondish guy is shaking the handle of his locker like he can't get the thing open. He glances over his shoulder as if he's embarrassed to be observed having this problem—especially when everyone should know their locker combination by now—and notices us looking at him. I toss a casual smile at him, but that only seems to embarrass him even more as he refocuses his attention on the stubborn lock.

"That's not him," I tell Olivia.

"That doesn't mean he's not around here somewhere," she points out. "Want to walk around school and see if we notice anything?"

"Sure." So we get sodas from the machine by the cafeteria and casually stroll around the school grounds, just sipping our drinks and talking. Who would ever guess that we're out here looking for trouble?

"Seems fairly quiet," Olivia says as we finish our rounds.

"Pretty dead, if you ask me." I glance at my watch now. "And I need to meet with Ebony, so I should probably get going."

"I'll catch a ride home with Alex today. I was going to his track meet anyway."

"Tell him good luck." I wave to her and then head out to the parking lot, still looking right and left and expecting to walk up on a group of thugs at any given moment. But there aren't any to be seen. I know I should be relieved or even happy about this, but I'm not. I feel as if I've missed something. And I'm even more concerned about the kid getting picked on or brutally beaten. Still, I know better than to obsess and worry. Instead, I pray for him as I drive across town to the precinct. God knows who this kid is and how to help him. I'm just a small part of that process.

"How are you doing?" asks Eric as I enter the police station. Eric is a good-looking guy who works with Ebony sometimes. He doesn't wear a uniform, and if you saw him on the street, you'd never guess he was a cop. In some ways he reminds me of my brother, Zach.

"Okay," I tell him.

"Ebony's in her office," he says with what seems a knowing smile. Eric is one of the few officers who know about my gift. And I suspect by his expression that she's already told him about my latest dream. Maybe he's been helping her do some research.

Ebony seems eager to see me. She quickly greets me and then gets straight to business. "First of all, you should know that there have been some terrorist threats to the Portland metro area recently."

I nod, trying to take this in. "You mean terrorist threats from outside the country?"

"Actually, we think they're insiders but obviously related to al Qaeda or the Taliban or someone in the Mideast who hates us."

"Why Portland?"

"Why anywhere?" she says with a deep sigh. "I suppose it's because we're one of the larger cities on the West Coast. A major port city. Any number of crazy reasons. Does it ever make sense?"

"I guess not. But why are you telling me this?"

"I'm wondering if it might have something to do with your dream last night."

"But my dream involved guns, not bombs."

"According to our sources, guns will be involved."

"But it still doesn't make sense," I tell her. "These kids were my age. Why would a terrorist have any interest in them?"

"According to our sources, the target won't be typical."

"Who *are* your sources?"

Ebony just smiles, and I know that means it's classified. But I can't help feeling curious.

"The point is that we're on high alert in the Portland metro area, especially when it comes to any group events. And particularly those that involve students. That has been made crystal clear."

"But why students?"

"How about if I read a portion of the threat to you, Samantha?"

"Can you?"

"Yes." Ebony turns to her computer screen now, pulls up a document, and begins to read. "'The execution will eliminate a small portion of immorality of the next generation, but it is a beginning.'" She sighs loudly. "Then they go on about reaping what we sowed and how judgment is coming and how they will be rewarded for killing. But between the craziness, it seems obvious to everyone that the threat specifically targets teens."

"Oh…"

"So given the fact that your vision was about high school students at an event that we can only assume was a prom, we have to put two and two together and take it as a serious possibility."

I nod. "Right…"

"So are we ready to move on?"

I nod. "Absolutely."

Now she points to a wipe-off board with what looks like a list of the high schools in our area. "These are the schools within the Portland metro area that haven't had their proms yet.

dates at the top—as in top priority."

"Wow, North Shore has one tomorrow night."

"Yes, that's the school we're focusing on right now." Then she has me go over all the notes from my dream with her again.

"Would you recognize this girl if you saw her?"

"I think so."

Ebony hands me a blue and white yearbook. "Start looking."

So while Ebony does some searching on her computer, I scan the pages of the North Shore High annual. But after nearly an hour of page after glossy page, I feel confused and frustrated. Every pretty blond girl is starting to look exactly the same to me. If only I could see her in that dress, with her hair like that…or those earrings…I know I'd recognize her then.

"This isn't working," I finally admit, closing the yearbook.

"I was afraid of that."

"But what if that girl is in here? What if I missed her?"

"I have a plan, Samantha."

"Okay…"

"What are you doing tomorrow night?"

I nod as I begin to suspect where she's going with this. "Do I get to do some reconnaissance?"

"Yes. My plan is for you to go to the North Shore prom. Are you up for that?"

I laugh. "What? I just walk in, and no one notices—"

"Of course, you'll have to go incognito. You'll be dressed for the prom."

"But I'm going stag?"

"No…I've asked Eric to escort you."

"Eric?"

"Yes, I think he can pass for a high school guy, don't you?"

I consider this. "Yeah, I suppose so."

"And that way he can be ready if anything starts to go down."

"Right…" The disturbing image of the splattered blood on the mint green formal gown hits me again. Combine that with the terrorist threat, and this is serious. Very serious.

"Are you okay with this?"

"Of course." I nod, hoping to appear confident.

"I'll be there too."

"Huh?"

"I'll pretend to be an employee at the hotel. Along with a few others. They're having the prom at a Marriott in northwest Portland, a hotel which happens to have white marble floors in the lobby."

I feel my eyes widen. "Really?"

"Yes. We've already been there, Samantha. Without giving away too much, I've spoken to the manager, and it's all set."

"Wow."

"And the FBI is aware of what's going on as well."

I nod, still taking this in.

"Are you sure you want to do this?" she asks with concern in her dark eyes.

"Of course."

"And just so you know, I've already spoken to your mother as well."

"Did you tell her about my dream?"

"Not the details… I'll leave that to you. I just wanted to make sure she was okay with this before I asked you to be involved."

"Was she okay with it?"

"She seemed fine. She really has great confidence in you, Samantha. And of course, I assured her that we wouldn't let anything happen to you. Mostly, I just want to get you in and out. You affirm that it's the right prom when you find the girl from the dream, and we'll take it from there."

"But what if she's not there? What if this is the wrong prom?"

"That's a possibility. But it's also a possibility that it's not the wrong one. And that's a chance we're not willing to take."

"Me neither." Suddenly I remember the vision I had earlier today, and I get out my notebook and share the details with Ebony. "I don't know if it's related to the dream though."

"What's your gut feeling?" she asks with concern.

I shrug. "I honestly don't know. I mean, I'm not trying to downplay the whole bullying thing, but in light of this terrorist threat, well, I suppose it seems less critical." I close my notebook. "I also know that God is the only One who can make it make sense. In the meantime, it seems like I need to focus my energy on this possible terrorist attack." I shudder to think of armed terrorists crashing a high school prom and senselessly shooting those in attendance.

Then Eric joins us, and after an hour we've worked out most of the details, including our fake names and believable explanations as to who we are and why we're at the North Shore prom—in case anyone asks. I will be Betsy, a new student, and Eric (a.k.a. David) is my college-aged boyfriend.

As I drive home, it hits me. I will be going to my first prom tomorrow night. But not Brighton's prom. And not with Conrad. I wonder if he'd feel bad or be jealous if he knew I was going to a prom with Eric. No, of course not. It's not like this is a real date. This is work—crime-solving work. Although I can't deny that Eric's a good-looking guy, and it'll be fun to see him in a tux. Still, I'm not taking this lightly. Most of all, I just want to prevent what looked like a gruesome murder—possibly one where terrorists are involved. That thought sends a serious shiver down my spine. But I know God will protect me. Still, this whole thing needs to be wrapped in lots of prayer.

Who knew you could rent a dress?" says Olivia as I turn into the parking lot at the strip mall Ebony told me about and stop in front of what looks like a normal formalwear store.

"Weird, huh?"

"Well, considering that you're wearing the formal as a disguise, you could think of it as more like a costume rental."

I've already told Olivia about tonight's assignment. She's one of the few people I can usually confide in—not always, but most of the time. And one of the main reasons I like having her in the loop, besides that she's totally trustworthy, is because I know she will pray. Olivia takes prayer as seriously as I do.

"Do you think they clean the dresses between rentals?" I ask as we get out of the car.

She laughs. "Of course. I'm sure there must be laws about things like this. Guys rent tuxes all the time, Sam. And I'm sure they're professionally cleaned."

Feeling relieved, I push open the door and see rack after rack of gowns. "Wow," I say as I look around the colorful room. "There are a lot of dresses here."

"Looks like they're organized by size," Olivia says as she begins to peruse a rack of size eights. She pulls out a red dress with sequins and holds it up. "How about this little number?"

I laugh. "A little too red for my taste."

"But with your dark hair, you'd look good in red."

"Thanks, but no thanks." I pull out a light yellow dress and hold it up.

"No," says Olivia with a firm shake of her head. "That is definitely not your color."

"Remember, this is just a costume," I say quietly.

"Even so, you don't have to look sick. And that yellow makes you look anemic."

"Oh…" I put the yellow dress back on the rack.

Finally we decide that my gown must (1) be a color that doesn't draw too much attention, (2) be a comfortable style with no cleavage showing, and (3) have a full enough skirt that I could run for my life if necessary. We narrow the selection down to eight gowns and finally decide on one that Olivia calls periwinkle but I call purplish blue. The color seems to change as I move around. Olivia says that's because it's iridescent. The dress is sleeveless but not the kind with skinny straps, and the neckline isn't too low.

"That empire waist should make it really comfortable," Olivia tells me. "And the skirt has plenty of room to move."

"But how does it look?" I ask as I peer at myself in the three-way mirror. Suddenly I realize that even though this is a working dress, I do want to look pretty.

"Beautiful," she says. "You look like a princess."

I frown at her. "Princess as in a five-year-old playing dress-up?"

"No, as in elegant, sophisticated. I think you should wear pearls with it."

"Pearls?"

She nods. "I have some that I'll loan you."

"But I don't want to take any chances with something valuable."

"They're just cultured pearls that my grandmother gave me when I was twelve. I don't think they're that valuable."

After getting the dress, we go to Shoes 4 Less, which is next door. Olivia tells me this is a big mistake, that I should at least get decent shoes, but I tell her that Ebony gave me a pretty tight budget. "And they're only for one night," I say as we go inside.

I try on about ten different pairs of shoes and eventually settle on a pair of strappy sandals that are sort of pearly looking. Olivia likes the color but not the thick heels. "They look like old lady shoes," she points out as I walk around in them with my jeans rolled up.

"But I could run if I had to," I say quietly. "Remember this is a mission, not a fashion show."

"Yeah, yeah…but if we go to our own prom, you have to promise you won't wear those, Sam."

I laugh. "We'll see…"

"And no rental dresses either."

"Hey, I was just starting to see how sensible it would be to rent all my clothes."

She groans as we walk up to the cashier. "And when I think of all my hard work trying to educate you in the refinements of fashion and style…"

"Yeah, right." I laugh as I set the shoebox on the counter. Just then I notice a guy emerging from the men's section. He looks slightly familiar, but as he glances at us, there's no recognition in his eyes. He's not very tall, not very well dressed, with wavy, sandy-colored hair and glasses. I stare at him and try to remember how I know him. And then, just as he exits the store, I realize he's the kid I saw getting beat up in that vision. I fumble for my money to pay for the shoes, and the cashier takes way too long to ring up the purchase, then bag the shoes.

"Come on," I say to Olivia as I grab the bag. "Let's go."

"What's the hurry?"

I rush outside and look around the parking lot, but it's too late. He's gone. Then I notice a bus pulling away from the curb and wonder if he might be on it. "What time is it?" I ask Olivia, reaching into my purse to pull out my notebook.

"Twelve twenty," she says. "Why?"

As I write down the time and location of this bus stop, I explain about the guy, reminding her of yesterday's search for the kid in my vision.

"That was him?"

"I think so."

"I barely saw him."

"Hey, maybe we should follow that bus," I say, "and see where he gets off." But by the time we get in the car and reach a busy intersection where the bus might've turned, I have no idea which way it went.

Olivia gets her phone out. "I'll call mass transit," she says, "and ask where that bus is headed." But when she calls, she is immediately put on hold, and by the time she gets a live person, who's not even helpful, I'm sure it's too late.

"How about lunch?" I say as I spot a Baja Fresh on the next corner. She agrees, and I pull in and park, then let out a long sigh. "I wish I'd been more with it. It's like I had this chance and I blew it."

"I should've been more help," she says as we go inside. "Next time something like that happens, just tell me what's up. If I'd known, I could've gone out and followed him. Or I could've paid for your shoes while you chased him down, Sam."

"Maybe it's for the best," I admit. "I mean, I should probably focus on this prom thing first. That's a much bigger deal. Not that I don't feel sorry for the kid being bullied, but his life didn't seem to be in danger."

"You're right. Solve this thing first."

Just the same, I call Ebony and leave her a brief message, simply stating the time and place where I believe I spotted the kid in my vision. As I hang up, I feel kind of silly. It seems like a small thing in light of this terrorist development. Besides that, the kid seemed perfectly fine. No black eyes or bruises or anything. Times like this make me wonder. What if I didn't get it right? What if I was getting mixed messages? All I can do is pray—and trust that God will lead.

After lunch, I take Olivia home, and we sit out in the sun and give ourselves pedicures and look at some of her latest fashion magazines. "I'm pretending that this is our prom night," says Olivia, pointing to a pale pink dress in the magazine, "and I'm wearing this."

I study the photo. "You know, that looks kind of like the dress in my dream. Only that girl's dress was mint green."

Olivia flips to the back of the magazine and peers at the fine print. "It says that this dress comes in pink peony, cream, and celadon green."

"What's *celadon* green?"

"It's a pale green."

"Like what I'm calling mint green?"

"That'd be my guess."

"Let's write this down," I say suddenly.

"Better yet." She rips out the page of the magazine with the information as well as the one with the photo. "Take these."

"Thanks."

Olivia loans me her pearl necklace and some earrings. "What about a bag?" she asks.

"Huh?"

"You know, an evening bag, for your cell phone and lip gloss and things."

"Oh yeah, right."

"I'll borrow something from my mom." Then Olivia takes off and returns with a pretty beaded bag in colors that actually look great with my dress.

"Thanks," I tell her. "Are you sure your mom won't mind?"

"Nah, she's got lots of them."

And then, because Olivia has band practice, I decide I should probably head for home.

"I'll be praying for you tonight," she says as we both get in our cars. "Keep me posted, okay?"

"Definitely."

"I'll be up late."

I nod. "I'll let you know how it goes."

"Be safe."

I wave to her. "Of course!"

But as I drive away, I wonder just how dangerous tonight might be. So far I haven't told my mom all the details of my dream. In fact, I got the distinct impression that she'd rather not hear them. And this morning she seemed perfectly fine about the whole thing. Like she actually thought I was going to another school's prom just for the fun of it. Maybe ignorance is bliss when it comes to my mom.

Knowing I might need it tonight, I charge my phone, first making sure I have both Ebony's and Eric's numbers on speed dial. Then to distract myself, I clean my room, which has been in serious need, and after that I actually do some homework. But while reading a boring section of text for U.S. History, I become seriously sleepy and decide I'm due for a nap. With the heavy book still lying open on my chest, I close my eyes and drift off to sleep.

When I wake up, I'm still in the grips of the horrible night-mare. It feels like I can't breathe, and I realize my history book is still on top of my chest. I shove it away and sit up, trying to calm myself, to breathe evenly…and to remember the details of that horrible dream. It was very similar to the last one: the same blond girl, same pale green dress, bright red blood splatters… Only just before I woke up, I saw what the girl was seeing—like looking through her eyes. Or perhaps only partly. I can't be sure. But in this dream I witnessed at least a dozen other kids, who all appeared to have been shot…all in formalwear…all on the same marble floor…some motionless as if dead…others crying out for help. It was ghastly. Gruesome. Terrifying.

With shaking hands, I reach for my phone, but before I can dial Ebony's number, it rings. I answer it with a hoarse-sounding "hello."

"Hey, Sam," says Conrad's voice. "You okay?"

"I just woke up," I admit. "I was sort of having a nightmare."

"Good thing I woke you then."

I start to explain that he didn't wake me, but then wonder, why bother? "What's up?"

"Just checking to see if you want to go to youth group with me tonight."

"I do…but I can't."

"Oh…"

I hate to lie to Conrad, but I can't tell him the whole truth either. "I already promised to go to this…this thing," I say, grappling for some believable explanation that's not a lie. "It's with an old friend of my dad's. She actually used to be his partner on the force, and I told her I'd go with her tonight. So I don't see how I can get out of it." Then I remember something. "Hey, isn't it supposed to be bring-a-friend night at youth group? Why don't you invite someone else to go with you—like Garrett or Jack?"

"Great idea, Sam. I'll give them both a call."

"Cool."

"We'll have ourselves a guys' night out." He laughs.

"Awesome."

"Are you busy tomorrow?"

I consider this. Hopefully tonight will go smoothly and life will be back to normal by tomorrow. "I don't think so. Why?"

"Just thought maybe we could do something after church. This weather is so great. Maybe something outdoors."

"That sounds fantastic."

"Cool."

We talk a little longer, and by the time I hang up, I no longer feel totally freaked by my bad dream. Still, I need to take it seriously. I carefully write down the details before I forget and then call Ebony on her cell, since I know she's probably not at the precinct on a Saturday. But my call goes straight to her messaging. Even so, I describe the details of my most recent dream, explaining that I feel certain a gun, or guns, are involved. But as I say this, a definite chill goes down my spine.

"It really did seem like it could be a terrorist attack," I finally admit. Then I hang up. It's nearly six o'clock now. Eric will be here in an hour to pick me up. Our plan is to arrive at the prom slightly early, which although a nerdish thing to do, is also a good way to keep an eye on things…hopefully to prevent something before it has a chance to start.

I pray as I get ready for my "big" night. I also apply several layers of antiperspirant. This could be a long evening. Then before slipping my cell phone into the beaded bag, I call Olivia and tell her about my most recent dream and ask her to pray.

"Oh, man!" she exclaims. "That's freaky scary, Sam. Are you sure you should even go tonight?"

"Hopefully, it won't happen," I say with a confidence I don't feel. "My purpose in going is to make sure that it *doesn't* happen."

"I will really be praying hard tonight. I wish I could ask the whole youth group to pray for you too."

"Maybe you can," I say. Then I explain what I told Conrad and suggest she could ask for prayer for me because I'm doing something with my dad's old partner. "You could say it's really important that things go right tonight. Something sort of vague but pressingly urgent."

"You got it."

"Well, Eric should be here any minute."

"How do you look?"

I stand and stare at myself in the full-length mirror on my closet door. "Okay…"

"Just okay?"

"Hang on, I'll send you a photo," I say as I hold my phone at arm's length and take a shot of myself. Then I wait for her response.

"You look gorgeous, Sam. And you put your hair up just like I showed you."

"Sort of. Anyway, I tried."

"Well, have fun…if that's even possible. And I know God is watching out for you, but do be careful. I'm praying!"

I thank her and promise that I'll be careful, then go downstairs where my mom gets all teary eyed when she sees me. "You look so pretty, Samantha," she says as she runs for her camera.

I protest as she snaps shots. "This isn't a real prom," I point out.

"I don't care," she stubbornly tells me. "You still look beautiful, and you're not getting out of here without proof."

Just then Steven shows up. As usual, he's dressed like he just stepped off a photo shoot for *GQ,* and when he smiles, his teeth glow in what seems an almost unnatural white against his tanned face. But Mom is glad to see him, and now they both direct their attention at me. Of course, he has to make a bunch of flattering comments, which sound a little forced to me, and even more embarrassing than Mom's. I almost admit that this is only a rental dress and no big deal, but I can't blow my cover. So I just smile and endure their compliments until a black limo finally pulls up in our driveway.

"Wow," Steven says as he looks at the car, "you're really going in style tonight, Sam."

"See ya," I call as I head for the front door.

"Hey, don't you want Conrad to come in?" he asks with a confused expression. Fortunately, Mom takes over now, leading him to the kitchen while I make a quick exit without having to explain why I'm not going with Conrad tonight.

"Hey," says Eric, who is halfway up the walk, "what's the big rush? I was going to knock on the door and do this thing right."

"My mom's boyfriend is here," I say. "I don't want to have to explain this to him. He thinks I'm going out with Conrad."

"Right."

So we hurry back to the limo, and Eric opens the back door. Feeling like Cinderella rushing to beat the clock (although that was *after* the big party), I practically leap into the car, and he gets in behind me. To my surprise Ebony and several other plain-clothes cops are in there as well.

"I got your message," she says, "and I decided to bring in the forces."

Suddenly I feel uncertain. "There's still a chance this might not be the right prom," I remind her.

"Like I said, Samantha, there's a chance that it is. And we're not taking any chances."

Ebony goes over details as we're driven toward the city. "Eric has on a wire," she says, "so we'll hear all your conversation. But if by chance you get separated from him, which we don't plan on, and you see anything suspicious, just call me on your cell." Then she goes over the rest of the details, explaining where she and the others will be posted. "And the police forces in North Shore and Portland, as well as the FBI, are nearby as well. All are on high alert. And just so you know, they really appreciate our cooperation in this."

By the time the limo pulls up in front of the Marriott, I'm a bundle of nerves. I take several deep breaths, shoot up a silent prayer, then steady myself as Eric helps me out of the limo.

"By the way," he says as we walk to the entrance of the hotel, "you look lovely tonight, Betsy."

I grin. "And you look pretty hot yourself, David."

"We'll be the mystery couple tonight."

"Where do you go to college again?" I say, just in case we have a conversation and someone asks.

"Portland State."

"Right." *I can do this,* I tell myself as we go inside. *With God's help, I can do this.*

ric (a.k.a. David) handles the tickets, and then we even pose for a photo beneath the starry arches before we go into the ballroom where the prom is being held. There are only a few couples, and I suspect some of them are on the committee and are there to make sure all goes well. Apparently the theme tonight is Hollywood and the red carpet. I'm not sure how Eric and I fit into this, but at least I don't think we stick out too badly. I suppose we should've checked on this sort of thing before selecting our "costumes." Like what if the theme had been tropical paradise and everyone had come attired in hula skirts, sarongs, and Hawaiian shirts?

Eric and I pretend to admire the glitzy decorations, then eventually get some punch. Fortunately the girl at the refreshment table doesn't seem to realize that we don't belong here. I'm guessing North Shore High is big enough that she doesn't know everyone. Hopefully no one else does either. After what seems a long time, more couples begin to trickle in. Eric and I stay near the entrance, taking turns watching for the girl in the celadon green gown. And surprisingly, or not, no one even speaks to us. We get some curious glances, as if they're trying to place us, but for the most part we are ignored. Maybe prom crashing isn't that unusual after all.

"Here comes a possibility," Eric says as he takes me by the elbow and, almost as if we're dancing, gracefully switches positions so I can see a blond girl in a light green dress.

"Close," I tell him, "but that's not her."

The night seems to drag by, and more and more I feel that this is the wrong prom. To pass time, I call Ebony and tell her as much, but she assures me that none of us is going home until the prom ends at midnight and everyone else is gone.

"Don't worry," Eric says as we go to the dance floor again. We stay along the perimeter of the smooth, wood floor, close to the entrance so we can take turns watching for the girl in the green gown. "No one's going to blame you if nothing happens tonight, Sam. Just consider this good practice."

"Practice?"

"Yeah. I'm assuming we'll be attending more proms...until we hit the right one and prevent the shooting."

I let out a groan.

"Hey, most girls would think this is fun," he says, "getting dressed up and riding in a limo to a prom." He frowns. "Or is it me? Am I a bad dancer?"

I laugh. "No, not at all. You're a great date, Eric. It's just that it's kind of stressful, you know?"

"That's what being a cop is about, Sam. You should know that."

"I know...I do...but this is different. When it's my vision or dream, I feel like if nothing happens, people will think I'm some wacko who was stringing everyone along."

Eric laughs now. "We know you're not a wacko, Sam. We all have great faith in your gift. We've seen it before. So far you haven't been wrong."

I nod and glance uneasily toward the entrance. I just wish that girl would get here and we could get this over with. Then I think of something. "You know, Eric, in my dream, the shooting occurs on marble floors."

"The dance floor is hardwood," he says, "and it's carpeted over there."

"I know. The marble is in the lobby." I stop dancing now. "Maybe that's where we should be. Maybe the girl never makes it into the actual prom."

He's already guiding me to the entrance. "Let's get some fresh air, Betsy," he says to tip off Ebony. Of course, this reminds me that they've been listening to our conversation all along. I hope I haven't said anything too stupid.

We go out in the lobby now and sit on a bench that encircles a fountain so we can watch couples coming and going. After a while I notice that more of them seem to be going than coming. "I don't think this is the right night," I say again.

"But is it the right place?" asks Eric.

I look around the lobby now. "The floor is right," I admit. "But I remember strings of lights in the background."

He glances around. "I don't see any."

"I know…"

He looks at his watch. "Well, there's less than an hour left now anyway. We can tough it out, can't we?"

"Sure… So since we're stuck here, tell me, Eric, are you dating anyone?"

"Besides you?" he teases.

"Yeah, and don't tell my boyfriend, okay?"

"Actually, I have a girlfriend."

"Really? What's she like?"

He considers this. "She's pretty and smart. Her name is Shelby, and she'll graduate from college in June with a teaching degree."

"She's going to be a teacher?"

"Yeah. She actually wants to teach middle school."

"Wow, she must be a brave woman."

"She is."

"Well, that's good. I think you need to be brave to date a cop." I think about my parents…how my mom used to worry…how her fears were finally realized. I hope and pray that never happens with Eric and Shelby.

Finally it's midnight, and almost everyone is gone. We wait until we're certain this is not the scene of the crime in my dream. Back in the limo, everyone assures me it's not my fault, saying it's better to be safe than sorry. And then Ebony tells me that another prom is scheduled for next Friday.

"We've already checked out the hotel for it, and there's not a scrap of marble floor anywhere. But I think it'd be wise for you to go by next week and have a look at it just in case."

"So I don't have to dress up and go to that prom?"

"Not unless you see something that convinces you the location is right."

"The hotel tonight really seemed like the one in my dream," I say sadly. "Well, except for no strings of lights and the fact that the girl in the green dress never showed and I was basically wrong."

"So far the only thing we know was wrong was tonight's date," Eric points out.

"And," says Ebony, "there happens to be another prom right here one week from tonight."

"Which school?" I ask.

"McKinley."

I consider this. "Isn't McKinley in sort of a, well, not a very affluent neighborhood?"

"It's a somewhat blue-collar community."

"The kids in my dream seemed like rich kids," I admit. "And Olivia and I found what could've been the girl's green dress in a magazine. It was pretty spendy."

"Maybe that will make it easier to spot her at the prom," suggests Ebony.

"Maybe...but it seems unusual that a girl from McKinley would have an expensive dress."

"Maybe she has a rich uncle...or maybe she rented it."

I sort of laugh. "I didn't see any dresses that nice at the rental place."

"Even so, why don't you get me the information on the dress, and I'll see if I can find anyone in the Portland area who carries that particular dress and try to track down someone who's purchased it."

"So, Sam, do you want to do this again?" asks Eric.

"Sure," I say, feeling unexpectedly hopeful. "I definitely want to prevent the shooting."

"And that gives us a whole week to do some more snooping," says Eric.

"Hey, maybe I could head over to McKinley," I offer. "Just look around and see if I can spot that girl or even the guy."

"That'd be great," says Ebony. "I wouldn't want you to miss much school, but maybe you could get excused for a day."

"Sounds good," I tell her.

"How about Friday?" she suggests. "That way it will be fresh in your mind before the prom."

"Except that every other Friday is test day in chem class," I point out. "Not that I would mind missing that."

"How about Thursday then? If you do it later in the week, it will give us more time to gather information."

"I just hope I'm not wrong..."

Ebony smiles at me. "I know you're disappointed about tonight, Samantha, but you do know that we're all taking this very seriously. We take *you* seriously."

"I know..."

"By the way, I asked at the hotel if there was a theme for the prom, and their events coordinator said it was going to be casino night. Sounds like it's going to be pretty colorful."

"High rollers," says Eric with a nod. "That should be interesting."

By the time they drop me off, it's settled. Same time, same place next week, hopefully with a different ending—and not a tragic one either. As soon as I get inside, I call Olivia. She sounds sleepy but curious, so I give her a quick update.

"I'm so glad you're okay," she says finally. "But I wish this was all over and done with."

"Me too," I admit. "Still, I need to see it through."

"Absolutely."

"I just wonder what I can use as an excuse for Conrad next weekend."

"Hey, which prom is this anyway?"

"McKinley."

"McKinley?" she shrieks in my ear. She suddenly sounds totally awake. "No way!"

"Why? What?"

"Because our band was just asked to play for McKinley. Cameron told us today. Apparently the band they'd booked totally bailed on them. They actually left the state and took the school's deposit money with them."

"Seriously? The Stewed Oysters are playing *that* prom?"

"Unless their prom committee finds another group they think is better. But Cameron sounded pretty sure. He has a cousin who goes there and told them about us."

"That's so weird." I realize this complicates things for me. What if a band member says something to blow my cover? I'll have to run it by Ebony.

"But cool." Olivia sounds happy now.

"Hey, do you guys do any Pretty Ricky songs?"

"Oh yeah, sure."

Goose bumps creep up the back of my neck as I recall the song in my dream. "It's pretty late," I say to Olivia. And it is definitely late, but the fact is, I don't really want to think about this anymore tonight.

"Yeah, I was half-asleep when you called. But I'm glad you're okay."

"Thanks." I hang up and hope we can get everything into place by next weekend. With God's help I believe we will prevent this.

The next morning I find my mom sitting at the dining room table surrounded by papers and punching numbers into a small calculator. "What's up?" I ask.

She looks at me with a tired expression, then removes her reading glasses and just shakes her head. "That's what I'm trying to figure out."

"Meaning?"

"Meaning, something isn't right with our finances, Samantha."

"What kind of not right?"

"I mean, there should be more money in my account." She gives me a slightly suspicious look. "You don't know anything about this, do you?"

"Huh?" I stare at her, feeling indignant. "What are you saying? You don't actually think I've helped myself to your bank account, do you?"

"No, no…of course not." She runs a hand through her messy bed-head hair, then frowns. "But what about Zach? Do you think he could've possibly done something?"

"I don't see how, Mom. He was in jail for two weeks, and he's been in rehab since then."

She nods. "Yes, you're probably right. It's just that I can't figure out where it went. My checking account was a little low, but I shouldn't have been overdrawn. What worries me most is that my checking is connected to our savings."

"So do you think your savings has been affected too?"

"It's possible."

"Do you have much in there?" I ask.

"It's not a fortune, but it's our safety net. Plus I've been stashing away what I could for your college tuition."

This surprises me a little. I had no idea Mom was putting anything aside for my education. She always acts like we barely get by, giving me the impression that I'll have to figure out college for myself or get some kind of magical scholarship.

"Do you think the bank made a mistake?" I ask.

"That's a possibility. I'll call them on Monday."

"And you don't do any banking online, do you? So it can't be some kind of Internet fraud?"

"I almost wish that I banked online now. At least I could've tracked this more easily. As it is, I'll have to wait until tomorrow to figure it out."

"What about identity theft?"

She sighs. "I wondered about that, but I hadn't used my debit card all week. It was only last night when Steven and I were in the city that I tried to get some cash from an ATM, and it showed insufficient funds."

"Maybe something was wrong with the machine."

"That occurred to me too. I'm sure there's a logical explanation. I'll deal with it first thing in the morning." She stacks the papers to one side, then looks up at me. "So how was your date last night?"

"It wasn't a date, Mom."

"Right… How was your undercover investigation?" She gives me a smirkish sort of smile. "Big drug bust?"

"No…just a bust, period."

"No arrests then?"

"Not last night. But we're going to try another prom next Saturday."

"Well, lucky you. Two proms. Do you get a new dress for the next prom too?"

Just in case she thinks that the Brighton Police Department is wasting precious budget dollars to buy me expensive prom dresses, I explain about the rental place. "But I suppose I could try something different next week," I say without mentioning that I'm actually considering a wig as well. I've decided I should probably go incognito now that it looks like Stewed Oysters will be there. No way do I want to explain to those guys why I'm at another school's prom with someone who's not even my boyfriend. This will definitely call for a real disguise.

Later that day, after church and a short hike with Conrad, I drive over to Olivia's house to take back her pearls and her mother's beaded bag. My plan is to invite Olivia to go with me to return the rental dress and hopefully pick out another one that I can reserve for next Saturday. But as I'm stopped at a quiet intersection, waiting for a woman in black sweats to jog across the street, I suddenly see a flash of light, and my actual vision gets blurred as something else appears in front of me. Instead of the jogger, I see a different person. Also dressed in black, it seems to be a man, and he's sort of hunched over in a sinister, cartoonish way, like he's trying not to be seen or sneaking away, or perhaps he's about to do something wrong.

For a moment I think I could be having a vision of a terrorist, maybe even one of the ones who plan to attack the McKinley High prom, but then he turns and looks directly at me so I can clearly see his face. To my surprise, it's not a terrorist but my mom's boyfriend, *Steven Lowery.* Then just like that—*poof*—the image is gone. I blink and shake my head and wonder if this was truly from God or just my imagination running amuck. Why would Steven be dressed in black and acting so goofy like that? Surely he's not the predator who plans to shoot innocent kids at a high school prom next week. That's just too bizarre.

I jump when I hear a horn honk behind me. Then I realize I'm just sitting at the stop sign with no cross traffic coming. So I put my foot on the gas and move forward, still trying to sort out what I just saw…or imagined. Very weird.

When I get to Olivia's, I tell her about this most recent vision, saying that it makes absolutely no sense. "I'm not that fond of Steven," I admit, "but I hardly think he'd shoot high school kids. And yet he seemed so sinister and evil to me. Not anything he did, but just a feeling I got. Silly, huh?"

"It does seem pretty strange."

"I wonder what it means… Was it a legitimate vision or something I just imagined?" I shake my head. "Sometimes I wish God would just rent a well-lit billboard or maybe a reader board. You know, print out whatever it is in bold letters to get His messages across. Much simpler."

"But God wants to use people to get His messages across, Sam."

I nod. "Yeah, I know. But sometimes it's confusing."

As we drive to the dress-rental place again, I tell her that I think I'll have to disguise myself for the next prom so the guys in Stewed Oysters don't wonder why I'm there or mention something to Conrad about me being with a different guy.

"Oh yeah, I hadn't even considered that."

"So I'm thinking a wig and some really wild makeup or maybe even sunglasses," I tell her. "It's a casino theme, so I suppose I could be a little over the top."

"I have a blond wig you could borrow," she says.

"Why on earth do you have a *blond* wig?" I frown at her. "In case you haven't noticed, you're *already* a blonde."

"The wig happens to have short hair." She laughs. "Remember when I was thinking about cutting my hair last spring? Well, I ordered this short wig online just to see what I'd look like."

"You never told me that."

"Because it looked totally stupid." She laughs. "The wig's style is right out of the fifties or sixties—like a big bubble head."

"Sounds perfect. And maybe I'll go for that flashy red dress this time."

"I'll have to tell the guys in the band about the casino theme," she says. "Maybe we can dress up too. This is going to be such a hoot, Sam."

I consider the irony as I pull up to the rental store. The fact that she's thinking this is all about fun and games when, in reality, I'm actually trying to prevent an extremely serious crime…well, it feels slightly twisted. Still, I have to agree with Olivia, it is kind of fun too. Crazy.

You don't think Steven has anything to do with the prom shooting, do you?" Ebony asks me after I tell her about my latest vision. "Any possible links to terrorism?"

"I can't imagine that he does," I admit. "But the image I saw of him seemed sinister."

"How do you feel about Steven...I mean, personally? Do you like him?"

"To be honest, I didn't like him at all to start with. But I guess I sort of got used to him. Do I *like* him? Probably not a lot. Still, he seems to make my mom happy. For her sake, I'm trying to be tolerant."

"And this seemed like an authentic vision from God?"

"Yes..."

"How about if I run a background check on him? Where did you say he moved from?"

"Southern California."

"That's rather broad. Did he mention a specific city?"

"I think he said he has a brother in San Diego and a mom somewhere else down there...but I can't remember him saying exactly where he's from."

"And you say he's an investment broker?"

"Something like that—insurance, investments, that sort of thing."

"Do you know where he works?"

I shrug. "No."

"Does your mom?"

"I'm sure she must." Now I frown as I remember something.

"What is it?" she asks.

"I don't know… I just thought of something… It's probably not even related." I sigh, then shake my head. "It's weird getting these messages from God and trying to figure out how they all fit together."

"Like a puzzle?"

"Exactly."

"That's what solving crime is all about, Samantha. We take lots of pieces. Some fit. Some don't. We keep trying to put them together until we can see the big picture. You're lucky, or I should say blessed, that God actually helps you with some of the pieces."

"Sometimes it doesn't feel all that helpful."

She smiles. "Yes, I can understand that." She picks up her pen again. "Now, anything else you can tell me about Mr. Steven Lowery? Do you know how old he is?"

"I'm not positive, but I do know Mom's about ten years older than him."

Her arched eyebrows lift slightly, but she doesn't say anything.

"I'm guessing he's in his early thirties."

"Well, that's a start anyway. And physical description? Hair color, eyes, height? And what kind of car does he drive? You don't happen to know his license-plate number, do you?"

I describe him as a young and less good-looking James Brolin. "Only his hair is lighter, but I think he gets it lightened," I tell her. "Kind of a Hollywood sort of look." Then I describe his car. "But I don't know his license-plate number. I could probably nab it the next time he's over."

"Great. I should have something on him in a couple of days."

At this point I come very close to telling Ebony about my mom's messed-up bank account. But I know that sounds pretty suspicious and accusatory. Besides, Mom said she'd check with the bank today. For all I know, the whole thing may be all squared away by now. Plus I'm sure Mom wouldn't be too thrilled about her private business becoming public knowledge. So I change the subject and tell Ebony about my scouting mission yesterday to the next prom site—the one with no marble floors. "It's not the hotel in my dream," I say finally. "At least I don't think so."

"Well, that's one we can take off the hit list." She makes note of this, then looks curiously at me. "Any more clues about that kid being bullied?"

"No, but I'm really praying for him. And I feel more certain than ever that he was the guy I saw in the shoe store on Saturday."

"I don't want to worry you," she says slowly, "especially with so much else on your mind. But I read a sad statistic just the other day..."

"About what?"

"About kids who are the victims of bullies."

"And?"

"It seems they are at serious risk. Being bullied was listed as the number one cause of suicide among teens."

I nod as I remember Garrett now, how depressed he'd been just a few months ago, how he'd even considered killing himself…mostly because his dad had bullied him. "Yeah, I can believe that."

"I'll be praying for this kid too," she assures me.

"I just don't understand why God would've shown me that vision if we weren't going to be able to help him somehow. Don't you agree?"

She nods. "I do."

"Well, I'll let you get to your work," I say.

"And I'll let you get to yours." She hands me another year-book. This one is for McKinley High.

Once again the plan is for me to spend a couple of hours carefully going through it to see if I can spot the pretty blonde or the guy who will be her date. And like before, I do my best.

But by the time I drive home, I feel slightly overwhelmed again. After two hours of carefully studying that yearbook, I didn't see one girl that I could be certain was the blonde in my dream. Eric even took the time to explain certain tricks to identifying people by their photographs. And I did manage to find a couple of girls who might be the one in the pale green dress, but I still feel rather doubtful. I also wonder if I'm going to be any good at this part of detective work.

Mom pulls up to the house just ahead of me, and I can tell by the way she's walking that something is wrong. She looks like there's a heavy weight on her shoulders. My first concern is for Zach. Is it possible that something's gone wrong in rehab? Could he have run away? I park my car in the driveway and hurry through the garage and into the house behind her.

"What's up?" I ask, making her jump. It's like she didn't even know I was there. "Sorry. I didn't mean to startle you, Mom."

"Oh…" She sets her purse on the island.

"Is something wrong?"

She lets out a loud sigh. "It didn't go well with the bank."

"Why's that?"

"They insist it's not their mistake."

"Oh…"

She lets out a long, weary sigh. "Not only that…but it seems the savings account has really dwindled as a result of being overdrawn."

I frown, curious as to how much money she's talking about but not willing to ask. She already looks upset. "What's next?" I ask.

"Now I have to go over all my records for the past six months and see what I did wrong."

"Are you sure you've done something wrong? Couldn't it be the bank's mistake?"

"They insist that it's very unlikely. They say that ninety-nine point nine percent of errors are made by customers, not them."

"But still, there's a chance…"

"A minuscule chance…and according to them, I have to prove I didn't make a mistake before they'll even look at their end of things."

"Oh."

"So that's what I'll be doing all night."

"I'll fix dinner," I offer.

"Thanks. I'd appreciate that."

While I'm working in the kitchen, Mom spreads all her papers and banking stuff across the dining room table once again, and before long she's punching numbers into a calculator and writing things down. I know she hates doing this sort of thing. She always has. And at times like this she really misses having Dad around. He was the one who always took care of finances. Consequently, I wonder if she might be a little careless in her bookkeeping. Not that I would ever mention this. Still, I feel sorry for her. And I feel sorry for myself too. The fact that the savings have shrunk—my college fund that I didn't even know I had—is pretty discouraging.

"How's it going?" I ask when she sits down to a dinner of green salad and lasagna (the prepackaged kind from the freezer).

She just shakes her head. "Maybe I should hand the whole thing over to someone who's better at this." She looks hopefully at me now. "Hey, you're pretty good in math, aren't you, Samantha?"

I frown. "I'm okay, but I really don't know much about checking accounts and banking and finances and stuff."

"Maybe I should ask Steven. He's a financial whiz."

I want to tell her I think that's a very bad idea, but I'm not sure how to say it without offending her. "Where does he work anyway?"

"What?"

"Steven. Who does he work for?"

"Oh, I can't remember the name. It's downtown Portland…a big firm with some long names." She sort of smiles now. "In fact, that's exactly what I'll do. He recently handled some pretty nice investments for me. Maybe I can hire him to sort this out as well."

"Investments?"

"Yes. He let me in on this fantastic opportunity, Sam. Within a year or possibly two, I will actually double my investment. Can you believe that?"

"How much did you invest?"

"Oh, not a lot, at least by his standards since he's used to dealing with some fairly wealthy investors. But it was my first time doing anything like this, so I was a little cautious. Now I think I should've invested more."

"Why?"

"Because at least my money would be safer there. I can't say as much for my bank. I'm tempted to switch banks altogether after this is over."

Okay, I am getting some pretty scary vibes right now. My mom's money problems and that vision about Steven seem to add up to nothing but trouble. And yet how can I possibly bring this up? "Where's Steven from?" I ask as I fork a chunk of tomato.

"Southern California," she says absent-mindedly.

"But where exactly?"

She looks at me. "You're sure getting curious about Steven all of a sudden."

"Well, you're pretty involved with him, Mom. Why wouldn't I be curious?"

"I think he lived in several places down there. I know he has a brother in San Diego, and his mom is in Pasadena."

"Oh…"

"You don't like Steven, do you, Samantha?"

I shrug. "I don't *dislike* him… I don't actually know him that well."

"But you suddenly seem suspicious of him."

I actually want to ask Mom why she's *not* suspicious of him. I mean, she's already questioned whether Zach or I had anything to do with her messed-up finances. But does she even stop to consider her mysterious boyfriend? She's entrusted him with her investments, but she doesn't wonder if he might have something to do with this? Is she that oblivious? Of course, even as I think this, I know my suspicions are pretty preposterous—not to mention slightly paranoid. And I'm not ready to make any accusations just yet. Still, I plan to let Ebony know.

"Thanks for dinner," says Mom as she returns to her book-keeping task.

I begin cleaning up the kitchen but find myself eaves-dropping as she talks on the phone. It sounds like she's leaving a message for Steven, telling him that she's trying to untangle her bank mess and asking if he would be interested in helping her. Then I hear her quietly say, "I love you," before she hangs up. This actually gives me the heebie-jeebies. *She loves him?*

I finish loading the dishwasher and then go upstairs to my room, telling myself that I should probably butt out of my mom's business. I mean, Steven might be a perfectly nice guy, and I could really stick my foot in it if I falsely accused him…but what about that vision? What was up with that?

So without hesitation I hit my knees, and I ask God to lead me through this maze of a life. And I acknowledge that just because I'm not overly fond of Steven, that doesn't make him a criminal. But if God is trying to show me some-thing, I do want to know. I want to be wise as a serpent… innocent as a dove. Finally I pray for Steven, that he would come to know God personally, that he would live the best possible life, both for his sake and for my mom's. And then I let it go.

I am running as fast as I can, so hard that my lungs are burning and I can't catch my breath. But when I turn to look, they are still behind me. Three guys, all bigger than me, and all look enraged. I don't know why they're so angry, but I have a feeling that if they catch me, I'll be dead. Or in a lot of pain. So I continue to run, turning down some sort of alley, but the next thing I know it turns into a dead end, a cement wall with a green Dumpster pushed up against it. If I can climb onto the Dumpster, I might be able to pull myself over that wall, but as I'm scrambling up, someone grabs me by the back of my jacket, pulls me down, and throws me to the pavement. A tall guy with dark hair, narrowed eyes, and clenched fists bends over me. "Thought you could get away with it, Allen. Thought you could outsmart us, didn't you?"

I just look at him speechlessly, holding up an arm to protect my face. But now they are punching me, kicking me, swearing at me, and yelling, "You're gonna pay, Allen!"

I wake up in a cold sweat. My heart is pounding with fear, and it takes me a moment to calm myself, to catch my breath, and to realize it was only a dream. I try to remember the details, besides the fear and the running and the useless attempt to escape. Why were those guys so angry at me? What had I done? And why were they calling me Allen?

I turn on the light and reach for my notebook. With my hand still shaking, I write these things down. As I write, I realize that I wasn't the actual victim in this dream. Oh sure, it felt like it.

But I realize that this Allen person is the same guy I had the vision about a few days ago, the same guy I saw at the shoe store. And he seems to be in real danger.

It's not even five in the morning…too soon to get up. And so I pray for Allen. I ask God to protect him and to send me more information to help him. I beg God not to allow Allen to be hurt like in my dream. I ask God to shield Allen from any possible thoughts of suicide, to keep him from giving up. And I ask myself, why are these guys picking on him? What has Allen done to make them so angry? Or are they simply bullies, picking on him because they can get away with it? My heart aches for Allen. Once again I plead with God to watch over him and to show me how I can help him. As I finally drift off to sleep, I wonder if Allen goes to my school. Tomorrow I will try to find out.

When I see Conrad on Tuesday morning, I can tell something is really wrong. At first I assume it might be because of me. It seems unlikely, not to mention slightly paranoid, but I wonder if he has somehow discovered that I went to a prom during the weekend.

"You look like you lost your best friend," I say as I meet him by his locker.

"I'm pretty bummed."

"What's up?"

"My parents got some new lab reports yesterday afternoon," he says, "regarding Katie."

"Oh no…" I put my hand on his arm. We've all been worried about his little sister this spring, and we've been praying for her to get well, but the last I heard, her health had improved. "I thought she was doing better," I say.

"We all did. But now the doctor thinks it might be lupus."

"What's that?"

He explains that it's a serious disease that causes low white-blood-cell count and can affect vital organs like the liver and kidneys. "My mom's taking her to see some specialist in Seattle tomorrow."

"I'm so sorry, Conrad."

"Yeah, it hit us pretty hard. Some kinds of lupus aren't that serious, but it sounds like it could be life threatening in her case."

"I'll really be praying for her."

"Thanks. My mom already put her back on the church's prayer chain."

Then the warning bell rings, and we head our separate directions to class. As I walk to the math department, I pray for little Katie. First I ask God to get her the best medical treatment available, and then I beg Him to do a miracle and actually heal her. I know God is able to do that. I pray that He does.

By the end of the day, all of Conrad's friends have promised to be diligently praying for his little sister, but I can tell he's still depressed. "I just don't understand why God lets stuff like this happen," he says as we stand in the parking lot to say good-bye.

I don't know how to respond to that. So I don't.

"Katie is just a little kid," he continues vehemently. "She doesn't deserve this crud!"

I nod. "I know…"

"Sorry," he says to me now. "I didn't mean to dump on you like that."

"It's okay… Sorry I don't have anything encouraging to say. But I do believe that God has a bigger plan, beyond what we can see. And I know He allows hard things to happen…but I also know He can bring good out of them too."

"Well, I can't see any good coming out of this."

"That's because you're in the middle of it, Conrad." I reach out and hug him now. "Hopefully, you'll see the good when you get to the other side of it."

"I hope so too. Thanks, Sam." Then he waves to Alex and Olivia, who are standing on the sidewalk. "I gotta get home, Alex. If you're coming with me, we better get moving, man." He turns to me. "You need a ride or anything?"

I point to my Bug. "No, I have my car today."

So we say good-bye, and Olivia and I get into my car.

"That's so sad about Katie," she says as I pull out onto the street.

"I know… It sounds like lupus is pretty serious."

"Alex said it's kind of like leukemia."

"We need to really be praying for her."

Olivia nods. "For sure."

Then we ride across town without speaking.

Olivia breaks the silence as I pull up to her house. "In light of Conrad's sad news, I wasn't going to tell you this…"

"Tell me what?"

"Alex asked me to the prom."

I smile at her. "Cool."

"He feels bad though, like maybe Conrad won't want to go now…you know, because of this thing with Katie."

"Oh, that's okay," I say quickly. "I'll probably be all prommed out by then anyway."

"I figured you'd understand."

"Of course."

And I do understand, but I also feel sad as I drive over to the precinct. I wonder why Conrad and I both have these grownup sorts of things to deal with. Why can't we just enjoy being regular teens, doing regular things, having fun and not worrying about such heavy stuff? But then I realize I wouldn't trade my life with anyone. Not really. However, I'm sure Conrad would do anything to trade his circumstances—that is, if he could do it in a way that would make his little sister well again.

"Hey, Sam," says Eric when I go inside. "How's it going?"

"So-so," I admit.

He nods with an empathetic look. "Still on for our date Saturday?"

"Oh yeah…"

"Ebony's looking for you."

"Thanks." Then I head down the hallway to her office.

"Have a seat," she says as soon as I enter.

"What's up?"

Her expression is hard to read. "I've been hitting some roadblocks in my investigation of Steven Lowery." She holds up a notepad with his name printed on it. "Is that the correct spelling?"

"Yeah."

"And you say he works for an investment brokerage in Portland."

"Something like that."

"Well, I'm not finding anyone by that name."

"And?"

"And I'm wondering if that's really his name."

"Why wouldn't it be?"

So she explains how things don't seem to be adding up, that he should be licensed as a broker either in California or Oregon. "And based on that, it should be easy to find information on him. But when I plug in his name, according to the description you gave me, I get nothing. And that worries me."

That's when I tell her about my mom's banking troubles.

"When was the last time your mom saw him?"

"I don't know. I mean, they went out on Saturday. And she called him last night."

"So he's still in town."

"Yeah. I guess so."

"And you don't know where he lives?"

"No…"

"Does your mom?"

"I assume she does…but I don't know."

"How about his phone number? Do you have that?"

"No, but I could probably get it from my mom."

"Do that, Samantha."

So I call my mom at work, and as I dial, I try to come up with some way I can ask for his number without sounding too suspicious. But she's out, and I ask the receptionist if I can leave her a voice-mail message. By then I have what seems like a good story—and not completely untrue either.

"Hey, Mom, I was visiting with Ebony just now," I begin in a careful but casual tone, "and I told her about Steven's great investment opportunity, and she wondered how she could get hold of him to find out more, but I don't know his number. Would you mind giving Ebony a call?" I leave Ebony's number and hang up. "How's that?"

She smiles. "You're good."

Then I tell her about last night's dream and how I looked for Allen at our school but came up empty.

She encourages me to use their database to see how many Allens fitting his age and description might be living in the greater Portland metro area. Naturally, there turn out to be a couple hundred teenage boys named Allen, and I feel more lost than ever by the time I quit. Detective work can be interesting, but it can also be just plain hard work. Finally I realize it's time to go home. I stop by Ebony's office to see if my mom called with Steven's number yet, but she's not around. I don't see Eric either, and I wonder if they're out working on a case or have simply called it a day.

As I drive home, I think about my mom and Steven. Should I try to broach the subject with her or simply wait until Ebony finds out something? Then I wonder what I'll do if Steven is there like he often is after work. What will I say? How will I act? Finally I decide I should be careful not to let him know I'm suspicious. Still, it would be nice to get a little more information out of him. Like where does he live? Where does he work?

When Mom gets home, I ask her how the banking fiasco is coming, and she admits that she has shoved it to the back burner. "There was a lot going on at work," she says. "I had my mind on other things."

"Have you heard back from Steven?"

She frowns. "No, he hasn't returned my call. He's probably having a busy day too. Hopefully, he'll stop by."

I nod. "Yeah...hopefully."

Then as I get a soda from the fridge, I overhear her calling him again, leaving another message. When she hangs up, I ask if she got my message at work.

"Yes, just before I came home. I called Ebony and gave her his number. I'm sure Steven will appreciate me finding him more investors." She sort of laughs then. "Hey, maybe I'll get a commission."

I try to look like this is a possibility, but at the same time I'm wondering how my mother can possibly be so naive. Still, it seems better not to question her. I take my soda up to my room, telling her that I have homework, which is true.

"I think I'll get a pizza delivered," she says.

"Sounds good."

"I'll call you when it gets here."

About an hour later Mom announces that the pizza is here. But I'm surprised to see she ordered a big one. "Expecting company?" I ask as I sit at the island across from her.

"I'd hoped maybe Steven would stop by, you know, to help me with the bank mix-up."

"Has he called?" I ask as I reach for a slice.

"No, and that's got me worried. He usually returns my calls right away. I hope nothing's wrong with him."

"Like what?"

"Well, there's a bad flu bug going around."

"Have you ever been to his place?" I ask.

"What do you mean by that?" She frowns at me.

"I mean, have you seen where he lives? Like is it an apartment?" I persist. "Or a house or what?"

"I haven't been there…"

"Oh."

"And if you're insinuating that he and I have been, well, you know…" She gives me a look. "It's really none of your business."

"I wasn't insinuating anything of the sort," I say defensively. "I was just curious as to how much you really know about him."

"And why is that, Samantha?"

"I don't know…but it seems a little mysterious."

"In what way?"

"So, you don't know where he lives or where he works, and yet you let him invest money for you. Don't you think that's a little odd?"

"I think your job at the police station makes you overly suspicious of people." I can tell she's mad now as she puts a couple of slices of pizza on a plate and stands. "And I think I'd rather eat by myself than with a daughter who makes accusations about a man I am seriously involved with. It was bad enough having Zachery turn on me, Samantha, but I expected better from you." And then she walks out and heads upstairs to her room.

So much for my wonderful sleuthing skills. Now I just hope that Steven doesn't show up tonight, because I'm pretty sure Mom would tell him what I said. Time to lie low.

Because she has a dentist appointment, Olivia and I take separate cars to school on Wednesday. After school ends, I go straight to the precinct, straight to Ebony's office, and I tell her the whole story of how I made what Mom called "suspicious accusations" last night, how she got mad at me for questioning Steven, and how she still wasn't talking to me this morning.

"I really blew it."

She sort of nods, but her expression is slightly grim.

"What's wrong?"

"Your mother left Steven's cell phone number at the office for me," she says. "I only got to it a couple of hours ago."

"And?"

"Does the name Greg Hampton sound familiar?"

I shrug. "Not really. Should it?"

"I discovered that the number your mother gave me for Steven is actually under Greg Hampton's name."

"Who's Greg Hampton? A friend of Steven's?"

"That's what I'm trying to find out. Want to see some photos I just pulled up?"

"Of Greg Hampton?"

"Yes, or a.k.a. Steven Lowery, whichever the case may be."

"Huh?"

"I think your mom's boyfriend may have changed his name a few times."

It doesn't take long before I spot a photo that looks exactly like Steven, or Greg, or whatever his name really is. I feel a mixture of relief and shock as I point to it. I'm relieved that I've finally been able to identify a person by his photo, but I'm shocked to see that Steven's real name is actually Gregory John Hampton. Not only that, but he's wanted in several states for fraud.

"Greg seems to have moved steadily westward," Ebony points out as she reads the details of the report. "His MO seems to be presenting himself as a successful stockbroker. Nice clothes, nice car, good-looking guy—quite a package."

"That sounds like Steven, or whatever his name is." I frown. "What does MO stand for anyway? I mean, I know it means the way a person does something, but what are the initials really for?"

She sort of smiles, but her eyes are troubled. "MO stands for modus operandi, and that's Latin for 'mode of operation'— the methods a person uses."

"Right."

"According to this, Steven's MO is to move to a new town and meet a vulnerable woman who possibly has money. He seems to prefer older women and widows. He begins dating them, wins their trust, promises them a great investment opportunity, then cleans them out before he heads on to his next target. As far as I can tell, he started this whole nasty business after 9/11. He targeted a policeman's widow in New York City. Apparently he has just the right sympathetic touch when it comes to tragedy."

I sink into the chair by Ebony's desk as I try to absorb this horrible news. "So he is responsible for my mom's messed-up finances?"

"That's my best guess. The big questions are if this jerk is still around and if we can catch him." She picks up her phone now, quickly dispenses some information, issues an APB for him, and then enters something into her computer as well.

"What about my mom?" I ask weakly.

She nods. "I'm going to go see her myself. I don't think this is something you need to handle, Samantha."

"She's going to be crushed."

"It's good that she has you…"

I nod, wondering if that's how Mom will see it. Or will she think this is somehow partially my fault? I know that seems completely unreasonable, but I remember how defensive she became over Steven last night. Like he was such a wonderful guy and I was somehow disloyal for questioning his integrity. Hopefully, she'll believe Ebony.

Seven

'm not mad at you, Samantha!" yelled my mom. Okay, her
tone wasn't exactly convincing. Nor was the fact that she'd
been slamming things as she supposedly cleaned up the
kitchen, which wasn't really in need of cleaning—just another
sign she was seriously ticked. But I wasn't about to argue with
her tonight. Instead, I slipped off to my room where I planned
to lie low until she calmed down—although it appeared that
might take a few weeks.

Naturally, she was not the least bit pleased with Ebony's
news. I'm not even sure she completely believes it. When she
came home after six, at first she almost acted like this was
some kind of conspiracy Ebony and I had cooked up against
her. Like we just wanted to make her life miserable. Then she
went into this "I'm not mad at you" rage, and I decided to stay
out of her hair.

My big mistake was getting hungry, which resulted in me
sneaking down to the kitchen. I thought the coast was clear
since it sounded quiet, and I wanted to get a little something to
eat. But when Mom saw me, she started ranting all over again.
So I retreated with my string cheese and orange juice back
to my room. Do I think this is fair? Of course not. But just the

same, I do feel for my mom. I know she's hurting and frustrated. Still, as I pointed out, she would be much better off if she could simply give this whole thing to God. He's the only one who can really sort this stuff out.

At least Olivia proved a sympathetic listener. Aggravated by my mom's immature reaction to the unfortunate news, I told Olivia the whole story, and she was incredulous.

"Your mom needs a good lawyer," she told me. "Go after that loser and make him pay her back."

"Yeah, Ebony pretty much said the same thing. And she definitely will do that, but in the meantime she's enraged and impossible."

"I'll be praying for her," promised Olivia. "And you too."

Her empathy was encouraging, but now, as I feel somewhat trapped and lonely up here, I decide to call Zach. After all, he may be messed up, but he's part of this family. And it might encourage him to know that his instincts about Steven were right on.

"No way!" he exclaims after I quickly relay most of the story. I don't go into all the details of how much money Steven stole from us, since I don't want to upset Zach too much.

"Pretty unbelievable, huh?"

"I always got a bad feeling from that guy. Remember how he was all over my case when we took the ski trip?"

"Well, to be fair, you kind of deserved it."

"Maybe…but not from him."

"That's true."

"How's Mom taking it?"

"She's in a rage."

"Figures. You can't really blame her."

"So how are you doing, Zach? How's life?"

"Pretty good. This is a really great place."

"Fantastic."

"Good people and good stuff." He pauses. "I was going to write you a letter, but I guess I'll just tell you now."

"Tell me what?"

"I totally recommitted my heart to the Lord, Sam."

"That's so cool!"

"Yeah. I can see now that it's been the missing link all along. There's no way I can stay sober without God in my life. I need Him."

"That's awesome, Zach."

"I've been thinking about Dad lately."

"Yeah?"

"It's like I can sort of feel his presence, like he's nearby or something. Is that weird or what?"

"I don't think it's weird. My guess is that as you get closer to God, it will naturally—or supernaturally—make you feel you're closer to Dad too."

"Does that ever happen with you?"

"Yeah, actually it does. Lots of times I get this unexplainable reassurance that Dad's up there…that he's rooting for us, you know, kind of like he's cheering us on."

"Do you think he's cheering Mom on right now?"

"Yeah, of course."

"That's cool."

"Well, I should probably go," I tell him as I glance at the clock. "I know you're not supposed to be on the phone more than five minutes at a time."

"Yeah. But thanks for calling, Sam. I mean, I'm really sorry to hear about Mom getting hurt and everything. But it's kind of reassuring to know I was right about that creep. I guess I should be glad I'm not home right now. I'd probably do something stupid like hunt him down and just make things worse."

"We need to let the police take care of it."

"Yeah. Hopefully, that jerk will be behind bars soon…just like Tate."

"That's what I'm praying for."

"I'll pray too."

Then we say good-bye and hang up. It sounds quiet downstairs again, and I briefly consider going down and trying to make peace with my mom, but then I decide it might be better to wait until she makes the first move. I don't see any point in talking to her until she's ready. Who knows how long it will take her to get over this?

Maybe the only thing I can do to help is to pray for her. And hearing Zach say how he's realized his need for God does give me new hope for Mom. Sometimes it takes some hard knocks to get us to the place where we finally cry out to God for help. Maybe that's what will happen with Mom.

On Thursday I drive over to McKinley High. Ebony has arranged for me to be on campus for the entire day. I go to the office, where they're expecting me and have even prepared a fake schedule for me. I've studied the yearbook and am hoping that I'll see something to tip us off today. Maybe I can spot and even meet the girl who will be wearing the pale green dress later.

"You can't tell us what this is about?" asks the vice principal with obvious curiosity. "Not even a hint?"

"Sorry." I give him a serious look.

"Police business." He nods firmly. "Detective Hamilton assured us that you'd be keeping it under wraps."

"For now, at least."

"Well, good luck."

It's kind of interesting, at least to begin with, doing investigative work while incognito, but as the day slowly (very slowly) winds down, I almost forget that I'm not really at school. Also, I'm missing my friends and realizing how it feels to be the new girl at a school where no one seems to want to meet me. Not that I'm trying to make friends, but the kids here seem pretty self-absorbed. Of course, I'm sure my school would be the same way for a newcomer. This is a good reminder to me to be more friendly when a new student comes on campus.

By the end of the day, I feel seriously discouraged. I have not spotted the girl. And although I've eavesdropped on various conversations that seemed prom related, I'm not finding out anything that seems to be helpful or even terribly informative. However, seeing these students and remembering my dream, I feel more determined than ever to stop this. I cannot imagine what it would feel like to be here at this school next week if a number of the students had been brutally murdered over the weekend. Ebony said that if we had concrete evidence that McKinley was really the school in my dreams, we might be able to cancel or postpone the prom, but as it is, we don't know this for sure. It's as if our hands are tied. And I can't help but feel partially to blame.

As I drive back to Brighton, I try to make sense of my life. Rather, I try to figure out what God is up to in my life. For starters…this thing with Steven. Did God try to show me this before and I just missed it? My intuitions about Steven were negative from the get-go. As were Zach's. And yet I assumed it was just because I resented that he sort of monopolized Mom's time and attention. But maybe I wasn't paying attention. Maybe God gave me those intuitions as a warning. But so much was going on…the thing with Zach…and Felicity. How am I supposed to keep track of all these things?

Finally I realize that all I can do is simply give it back to God. I believe He made me…He gave me this gift…it's up to Him to sort it out. All I can do is be available and willing. Fretting over it will not help one bit. But prayer will. And so I decide to commit the rest of this afternoon to prayer. And as weird as it sounds, I go home and go inside my closet to do this. Jesus taught that we shouldn't make a big deal about praying, and we should never do it for attention. So I follow His advice and go into my closet and close the door, and to my amazement, it's very cool. And by the time I emerge, feeling slightly like a mole as I blink in the light, I am at peace. Somehow God is going to work things out. I believe this.

By Friday afternoon Conrad is so concerned about his little sister that he and Alex have decided to drive up to Seattle to pay her a visit in the hospital, where she's about to be treated with some new medication. "It's supposed to be really good," he tells us as we stand in the school parking lot. "But it's also somewhat dangerous. My dad said that it sounds like she'll either get a lot better...or worse."

"I told Conrad that this calls for a road trip." Alex pats him on the back. "We should be in Seattle by eight o'clock."

"Be safe," I say. "And tell Katie I'm praying for her to get totally well."

Conrad nods. "Will do."

Olivia and I wave good-bye as they drive off in Conrad's goofy-looking orange car. I hope it's roadworthy. If not, I'm sure they'll work it out. Maybe it'll be a good guy adventure. And Katie will appreciate it. I know how much she looks up to her big brother.

"At least you don't need to make up any phony excuses for not going with Conrad to youth group tomorrow night," Olivia says as we get into her car.

"Yeah, I hadn't thought of that. But I'm starting to miss youth group," I admit.

"Hopefully, tomorrow will be your last prom-crashing night. Have you got your costume all ready to go?"

"I haven't picked up the dress yet, but I tried on your wig last night. I even did the makeup the way you suggested."

"The blue eye shadow and false eyelashes and the works?"

"Pretty funny. I didn't even recognize myself. I almost went down to show Mom, you know, pretend like I was a total stranger. But I didn't think she'd appreciate it. Her sense of humor isn't too sharp right now."

"Is she still in a snit?"

"I think she's done with the anger part now. Ebony said it might be like she's going through the stages of grief."

"So which stage is she at now?"

"Denial, I think."

"You're not suggesting that she thinks Steven, or whatever his name was, is innocent, are you?"

"Sort of…plus she kind of blames herself."

"That is so weird."

"Tell me about it."

"I'm going dress shopping tomorrow," Olivia says as she pulls up at my house. "You want to come?"

"Sure. I need to pick up my dress for tomorrow night; maybe you can find something at the rental place."

She laughs. "That wasn't exactly what I had in mind."

"No, I didn't think so."

"How about I pick you up around eleven?"

"Sounds good."

"I'd ask you to do something tonight, but the band is having a long practice to be ready for the prom. This is our first prom, and I think Cameron is nervous."

"How about you?" I ask as I get my bag. "Are you nervous?"

She nods with a serious expression. "Yeah, but not about the music. I was thinking about your dream…and I even wondered about not going." She looks at me with concern. "Do you think it'll be the real deal tomorrow night?"

"I'm not sure. Like I told you, yesterday's investigation didn't turn up a thing."

"No more dreams or anything either?"

I shake my head. "No."

"So maybe it's not tomorrow night's prom?"

"I just don't know."

"It's not that I'm scared, Sam. Not really. But it's a little unnerving, you know, thinking that something like that could really happen."

"You know, Olivia," I begin slowly, "if you have a bad feeling about this…maybe you shouldn't go. I mean, I respect the fact that God does give us intuitions, and we really need to pay attention to—"

"No. I *want* to go. Nothing's going to keep me from going. But I guess I'm a little nervous. That's all."

"Well, the police will be all around the place. Security will be tighter than ever now. I'm sure we'll be safe." But even as I say this, I wonder how I can be so sure.

She smiles as I get out of the car. "Yeah. God will protect us."

I think about this as I go inside my house. I do believe that God will protect us, but I also know that bad things really do happen to Christians. I'm not stupid. And I am well aware that my dad died while trying to prevent a crime. And although it seems unlikely, I suppose something similar could happen to me as well.

Still, does that mean I should live my life differently? I don't think so. I think I'd rather live "dangerously," knowing I'm in God's will, than live "safely" outside it. Now *that* would be truly scary.

Eight

"I haven't heard a single word from Ebony," Mom complains on Friday night.

"What were you expecting to hear?" I cautiously ask as I get the pitcher of iced tea from the fridge. Mom sort of snuck up on me just now, and I think this is the first actual conversation we've had since she found out about her so-called boyfriend's secret life.

"That they've arrested Steven, of course."

I sense she's taken a step forward in her stages of "grief," but I'm not exactly sure where she's heading. "These things take time," I tell her in what I hope is a soothing tone.

"They should've caught him by now," insists Mom. "The longer they let it drag out, the farther away from here he'll get. He's probably out of the state by now. Probably already hitting on another unsuspecting widow. He needs to be stopped."

"I totally agree," I say as I pour a glass of iced tea. "So does Ebony. I'm sure everything possible is being done."

"But he's still out there, scot-free and spending my money!" Mom slams the cupboard door so hard that the dishes rattle inside.

I don't know how to respond to this, so I don't.

"The police are supposed to be public servants," she continues. "My taxes pay their salaries."

"Right…" I take a sip and watch as she plants both hands on top of the island. I want to point out that it's not much different than her job with the parks and recreation department, but I know that won't help.

"So, I want satisfaction."

I nod. "What would give you satisfaction, Mom?"

"Seeing Steven locked up for a long, long time. And making him pay me back. Not just the money he stole, but everything else too."

"What else did he steal?" I feel concerned now. Did I miss something?

"He stole my trust, Samantha."

I consider this. "How did he steal something you gave to him?"

"I may have given it, but he abused it."

I want to tell her that she should give that kind of trust to God, that He'll never abuse it. But I don't think this is the right time.

"And he stole my pride. Do you know how humiliating this has been?"

I shake my head. "But I can imagine."

"He made a complete fool of me. And for that reason alone, I think he should pay."

"I agree. I want to see him locked up too."

"I wish I could get my hands on him first," Mom says with a wicked look in her eye.

Okay, I probably shouldn't ask, shouldn't encourage her, but I am curious. "What would you do?"

"I'd make him sorry he ever met me. I'd think of a way to get even, a way to publicly humiliate him so badly he'd never want to show his face in this town again."

"I don't think he's too eager to show his face around here as it is, Mom."

"Sometimes I wish we could take the law into our own hands," she says in a vicious tone.

Now I don't honestly think my mother would ever resort to something like that, but just hearing her talk this way is a little unnerving. It sort of reminds me of Zach, but at least he's turning to God now. On the other hand, my mom seriously worries me, and not for the first time, I find myself wondering which of us is the adult here. Will the real parent please stand up?

"I know you're judging me, Samantha," she says a little more calmly.

"No…" I shake my head. "But I am trying to figure you out."

"Well, I'm a woman who's been wounded. Deeply. And it's going to take awhile to get over it."

"You know, Mom…," I begin carefully, "if I were in your shoes, I'm sure I'd feel the same way. I honestly don't see how you can get over something like that at all—without God."

"Yes, I knew I'd eventually get a sermon from you, Samantha."

"Nope. That's it. No sermon. Just a statement…a simple observation."

"Call it what you like." She turns and walks out of the kitchen, and I know that's the end of the conversation. But at least she's talking to me now, which is an improvement.

As is often the case with my mom when she's frustrated with life, she throws herself into her work. Consequently, I'm not surprised when she goes to work on Saturday morning.

And for a while I actually begin to feel the same bitterness that was coming out of her last night. This is all Steven Lowery's stupid fault. He has stolen not only our money but part of our lives as well. I hate him for doing this.

And then I realize that if I'm going to live out my faith, I will have to forgive him. I will have to extinguish that bitterness before it robs me of something far more valuable than just my college fund. And maybe I can't forgive him today, but I know I must do it soon. I also know that it will take God's help to forgive him. So as I'm getting dressed to go shopping with Olivia, I ask God to help me with it. I tell Him I'm willing but I'm just not sure I'm able.

"Are you worrying about tonight?" asks Olivia as she drives us to the mall.

"No…I was just thinking about my mom and this whole Steven thing."

"How's she doing?"

I explain how she's entered a whole new stage. "I think she wants to become a vigilante now," I joke. "I almost expect her to start saying things like, 'Hangin's too good for the lowlife, bottom-feeding, no-good jerk.'"

Olivia laughs. "Your poor mom. She's been through so much."

"I guess."

"You all have." She shakes her head. "Just last night my dad was saying how he really feels for your family. It seems like you guys get hit with one thing after another."

"Maybe it's like that old saying, what doesn't kill us makes us stronger."

"Then you should all be really strong."

"I think Zach and I are getting strong in the Lord, but Mom's putting up a hard fight."

"We'll just have to pray harder."

"Speaking of praying, Conrad called last night to say they made it safely to Seattle. Unfortunately, it was past visiting hours, but he plans to spend most of today with Katie."

"We should let someone in the youth group know," Olivia says. "They can be praying specifically for her tonight."

So as she's driving, I call the church and leave a message for our youth pastor about Katie. Then I add, "And you guys should also pray for Olivia since the band she's in will be performing at the McKinley High prom tonight. Pray that it goes well and that God will use Olivia there."

"Good thinking." Olivia snags a parking place close to Nordstrom's entrance. "Too bad you couldn't have them pray for your work tonight too."

"Not without blowing my cover."

"Well, I'll be praying for you."

Then we go inside, and for several hours I am just a normal girl, doing normal things with my normal best friend.

"I wish you were going to the prom with us," Olivia says as she models a gown that looks almost like what Cameron Diaz wore to the Oscars.

"You look gorgeous," I tell her. "That's definitely the best dress so far."

Finally she's made all her choices, including a pair of killer shoes, which will probably be killing her feet before prom night ends. Then we go for lunch at the food court. We're about to sit down when I see a familiar-looking figure.

"That's the kid!" I say as I practically drop my tray on the table.

"What kid?" asks Olivia, glancing around with a confused expression.

"Allen, the one in my visions who gets beat up all the time. I gotta follow him."

"I'll be right here," she says patiently. "My phone is on."

Then I take off. Not running, of course. I don't want to be too obvious. And I don't want to scare him either. I go after him, trying to think of some kind of plan. But I'm coming up blank. What do you say to a kid who you know is being bullied? What kind of answers can I possibly give him? I can't exactly say, "Hang in there. Things will get better." For all I know, they won't. Then I have to wonder why God gave me these visions in the first place. How am I supposed to help him? So as I follow him, I pray.

He goes into the video-game arcade, and acting like I do this all the time, I do too. But suddenly I'm wishing for Olivia. She knows video games lots better than I do. He goes directly to a machine with graphics of what appear to be gang members or street fighters. And he pops in a token and starts to play. I pretend to play a game that's a couple of machines over, but since I don't have any tokens, I can't even make it work. I can tell by Allen's score that he's good at the game. I wonder if that's how he deals with the fact that he's being beat up in real life—he takes it out on the video game.

Finally I decide to just walk over and watch. "You're really good," I say to him in a casual tone.

He doesn't even look up, doesn't say a word.

"If you don't want me to watch, I'll leave," I continue. "But I'm not very good at video games myself, so I thought I might learn something."

He barely glances at me, then continues to play. "You can watch if you want," he finally mumbles.

"Cool." So I continue to watch, and I compliment him and act like I think it's great that he can beat up all these guys on the video screen, even though I actually think it's kind of sickening. I mean, the graphics and sound effects on these games are way too realistic for me.

After what seems a long time, he's done. He turns and looks curiously at me. "Who are you anyway?"

I shrug. "Just an innocent bystander." Then I smile and stick out my hand. "My name's Sam. Short for Samantha."

He pauses, then shakes my hand. "I'm Brandon."

I try not to act surprised. I mean, I really thought his name was Allen. But maybe I was wrong about that. Because I know for certain this is the guy in my visions. I make some more small talk about the video arcade and how I'm just killing time before I meet my friend at the food court. Then I ask where he goes to school.

"Fairmont," he says.

"I go to Brighton. You guys creamed us in basketball this year."

"Yeah, we went to state."

"How'd you do?"

"Third."

"Not bad."

Then I see him looking at something, or someone, out of the corner of his eye. "I gotta go," he says quickly.

I glance over to see a couple of guys pointing at us and starting to make their way across the room. The next thing I know, Brandon takes off running and escapes through what turns out to be an emergency exit, setting off an alarm. I step in front of the two guys now, stopping them from following him. "What's up?" I ask.

"Who are you?"

"A friend of Brandon's."

The tall, skinny guy laughs. "Yeah, right."

"Are you guys picking on him?"

"What's it to you?" asks the shorter, blond guy. He has a bad complexion and eyes that dart nervously around. He tries to move past me, but I reposition myself.

"I said I'm his friend."

"That nerd doesn't have any friends."

"Why?"

"Because he's a geek."

"Is that why you think it's okay to pick on him?" I persist, trying to stall them long enough for Brandon to get away. By now an employee has come to check on the door, firmly closing it and stopping the alarm.

"We pick on him because he asks for it."

"I didn't see him asking you guys for anything."

"Come on, Reese," says the taller guy. "He's probably long gone by now anyway."

"Why don't you leave him alone?"

"Why don't you butt out?" says the tall guy.

I glare at both of them now. "Bullies are just cowards," I say, "trying to make themselves believe they're brave. You should just get over it." Then with a look of utter disgust, I turn and walk away. My heart is pounding, and for a brief moment I think they might turn on me now. But I doubt they'd be that stupid. What kind of idiots would try to beat up a girl in a busy mall like this? Just the same I open my cell phone and call Olivia.

"What is going on?" she demands.

"I'm on my way back," I say. "I'll explain when I get there."

"Well, your food is cold."

"That's okay," I say as the confidence returns to my steps. "It was way worth it."

I tell Olivia the whole story as I eat my cold slice of cheese pizza.

"Wow," she says, impressed. "You just saved him from getting beat up."

"This time." I sigh.

"But the way you told those thugs off...maybe they'll rethink their actions next time."

"Except that they're not the only ones who pick on Brandon." I get my notebook from my bag now and write down his real name and the school he attends. At least I got a little information. "Maybe Ebony can contact Fairmont to let someone in authority know there's a bullying problem going on."

"Yeah," she agrees. "That might be the whole purpose behind that vision, Sam. Just getting the right information to the right people."

I close my notebook and smile. "It does feel good to have possibly solved one case."

"Hopefully, you'll solve another one tonight."

"Or prevent one," I add.

Next we go to an accessories shop, and Olivia talks me into getting the cheesiest-looking rhinestone jewelry. Fake diamonds and rubies to go with my over-the-top prom outfit.

Then as we're driving home, after we've picked up my flashy red dress, I suddenly remember the pretty pale green dress worn by the girl in my dream—a dress like I might wear to a real prom, if I were ever asked. But that makes me wonder if all the McKinley kids will be dressed like that. What if this strange-looking getup I've put together is all wrong? What if, despite the casino theme, all the kids are wearing traditional-looking prom clothing? Won't I stick out? I mention this to Olivia as she pulls up at my house.

"You could always pretend you're dressed up like that because you're an entertainer," she offers.

"And then what? Go up there and sing? Badly and off key?"

She laughs. "Just go with the flow, Sam. I'm sure you'll be fine."

Well, I'm not so sure. But I thank her for the ride, tell her I'll see her in a few hours, and go inside to consider my fate.

Nine

My mom's still not home when it's time for me to go to tonight's prom. She hasn't called or left a message or even a note, and that worries me a little. I leave a note for her, telling her I'm with Ebony doing police work. However, as I check out my image before leaving, I look more like I'm doing vice work, and I'm somewhat relieved Mom can't see me.

When I get into the limo, I take some friendly teasing about my blond wig and overdone makeup. Ebony tells me I'd make a good Marilyn Monroe, which I think is sort of flattering but totally ridiculous. To change the subject, I fill her in on my encounter with Brandon today, explaining that he goes to Fairmont High. "And they have a prom coming up too," I point out.

"Hmm." She takes out her notebook and jots down something.

"Do you think there's a connection?" I ask with uncertainty.

"I think it's worth investigating."

"He seems like a nice kid," I tell her, suddenly feeling sorry for Brandon and hoping I didn't get him into more trouble with his tormentors.

"Nice tux," I say as Eric helps me out of the car. He's wearing a white satiny jacket with a black shirt underneath. "You look like you should be performing at a nightclub."

He laughs, then straightens his white tie. "I was going more for a Mafia man look."

"Do you think this will be the real deal tonight?" I ask Eric as he escorts me up to the Marriott hotel again.

"You're the one with the special gift," he reminds me.

"Well, this feels like a déjà vu to me. I just hope it's not another wasted evening."

"Me too. I'd like to get this thing wrapped up and locked down." He turns and looks at me, then laughs. "Not that you're not a hot date, Sam, but I already have a girl."

"Funny."

"I'm just ready to move on."

"Me too. This is getting pretty nerve-racking."

"And this whole Saturday night deal is not making Shelby happy. She really wanted to go to a movie tonight."

"Does she know what you're doing?"

"Sure. But she can be trusted."

Once again we're early. We casually walk around, casing the joint, checking out the band, who seem oblivious to us as they play warmup songs. Olivia is the only one who recognizes me, although she gives me a totally blank look. Her outfit, a hot pink sequined number, is almost as bizarre as mine, although her hair looks more natural.

Eric and I mostly hang close to the entrance, making small talk as we keep an eye on the newcomers. Then we wander out to the lobby anytime it starts to get busy. As more couples arrive, I'm pleased to see that the McKinley students have taken this whole casino thing to heart. Everyone is flashy and glittery and sort of over the top. Eric and I fit in just fine. And the girl in the pale green dress ought to be easy to spot if she's here.

Unfortunately, as the night wears on, we don't see that girl anywhere. But like last week, we don't want to give up too soon. You just never know.

"I really don't want to do this again," I complain to Eric, and he gives me a look that says he's had enough proms for a life-time too. We're sitting out in the lobby, and to my surprise I recognize someone. I nudge Eric, then nod to where Brandon, the kid who's been bullied, is standing near the registration desk. I briefly explain to Eric who he is and the visions I've had about him. I even tell him about the two bullies I stood off at the video arcade earlier today.

"I wonder what he's doing here," Eric says.

"I don't know," I say. "Obviously he's not here to go to the prom. Besides, he told me he goes to Fairmont."

"Do you think he's getting a room?"

"That would seem kind of weird, not to mention expen-sive." Something about the way Brandon is dressed—his less-than-fashionable jeans and unimpressive polo shirt, a beat-up, oversize backpack—suggests he's not exactly a rich kid.

Now Brandon is speaking with a gray-haired man working at the registration desk, and the man hands him something—it looks like a piece of paper or an envelope. Then Brandon leaves, but not through the front door.

"Interesting," Eric says. "Maybe we should check him out."

"Why?" I ask.

"Well, he was in your vision…and he's here tonight… Maybe there is a connection."

"Maybe…," I tell him, but I am doubtful. For one thing, Brandon doesn't seem like the prom type. Eric is already talking quietly, as if he's speaking to me, but he's actually describing Brandon and his whereabouts so the other surveillance cops can be in the loop. Still, I can't imagine Brandon wanting to have anything to do with a prom—and certainly not one where he doesn't even attend school. It just doesn't add up.

Even so, we keep watching for him, although I don't expect him to come back. I feel sorry for him as I remember those two guys at the mall today. Why do people act like that? "I just don't get bullies," I say out loud. "What makes some guys want to bully others?"

"Meanness." Eric blows out an exasperated sigh and glances around the thinning crowd.

"I guess. But why?"

"Probably that old cycle-of-life thing," Eric says. "Someone is mean to you, so you're mean to others, and it just goes on and on."

"The gift that keeps on giving."

He laughs and nods.

Yet I think he's hit the target. Meanness begets meanness. And this reminds me of my mom and her recent need for what she calls "sweet revenge" but what I think is actually bitter stupidity. I just hope she's not out doing something crazy right now. I overheard her talking to her friend Paula on the phone last night. She was being sarcastic, saying how they ought to go look for "that good-for-nothing Steven," saying how the two of them could teach him a lesson he'd never forget. I remind myself that Paula is a trained family counselor—okay, she's not a great counselor, and she drinks too much—but surely she'd know better than to do something like that. Besides, I'm pretty sure Steven Lowery is long gone by now.

"I think the party's over," Eric says in a tired voice.

"Yeah, it sounds like the Stewed Oysters just played their last song."

"No crazed terrorists that I can see anywhere."

I shake my head. "I'm sorry..."

"It's not your fault, Sam."

"I just wish I could get some clearer signals." I look around the deserted lobby and back toward the ballroom, which is also nearly empty. "What a waste of time."

Eric doesn't say anything as we walk back to the limo, but I think he's questioning my judgment. I'm sure they all are. I know I am.

"Don't blame yourself, Samantha," Ebony says as we pile into the limo again.

"How can I not?"

"It's time for us to get serious about looking into that Brandon fellow," she continues. "I heard you and Eric talking about him, and Eric's right. It might not be a coincidence."

"But he just came and left," I point out. "How does that mean anything?"

"I don't know, but I do know that Fairmont is having their prom next weekend, and guess what, people?"

"Same place?" I ask.

"That's right. Prom central."

"Oh..."

"So we're on again?" asks Eric in a tired tone.

"Afraid so," says Ebony. "I don't see how anyone can rest until we prevent whatever this is from happening." She sighs. "You all can see now why it wouldn't have worked to cancel any of these proms. Can you imagine the flak we'd take for that?"

"Or the flak we'd take if the terrorists actually make it through security," adds Eric.

"And Fairmont fits your profile better," says Ebony.

"How's that?" I ask, not sure I even care.

"It's in an affluent community, full of people who can afford the kind of dress you saw in your dream."

I nod as if that makes sense when I really just want to groan and complain and say, "No way can I endure another prom." But I know that would be immature. This job needs to be taken seriously. I just wish we could get to the bottom of it. I close my eyes and lean back against the cushy leather seat. *Please, help us,* I silently pray. *God, help us to solve this thing.*

When I get home, Mom's still not there. Staying out late wasn't unusual when she and Steven were dating, but it seems a little odd now. Still, I figure she's probably with Paula. Hopefully they're not out getting wasted. My mom promised me she wouldn't do that sort of thing anymore. Although with the way she's reacted to Steven's crud, I don't know if that promise is still good. Even so, I decide there's nothing I can do about my mom's life, and I go to bed.

The next morning my mom's still not home, and now I'm seriously worried. I try her cell phone, which is turned off. I try

Paula's number, and no one answers. So I leave a message, telling her that my mom never came home last night and that I'm worried. I consider calling Ebony but decide to wait. Maybe my mom's at Paula's house right now; maybe they're both sleeping off a night of overindulgence. I can only hope.

I go to church but cannot concentrate on the sermon because I am getting so worried about Mom. I leave my cell phone on vibration mode just in case she calls. But she doesn't.

"Are you stressed over last night?" asks Olivia when the service finally ends and I'm hurrying out to the parking lot. I quickly tell her about my missing mom, and although she seems concerned, she tells me not to worry. "She's probably home right now," she assures me. "You know parents… They expect to know where you are 24/7, but when it comes to their whereabouts, they can be pretty vague."

"Maybe…but it seems like she might at least call."

"Let me know how it goes," she says. "My parents are dragging me to my great-uncle's eighty-fifth birthday party down in Salem, but I'll have my phone on."

"For sure!" I wave, then hurry to my car. I am getting a really bad feeling about this. I pray as I drive. When I get home, Mom and her car are still not there, so I call Ebony.

"Where do you think she is?" Ebony asks after I've explained the situation.

"I don't know…but I have a bad feeling…"

"What sort of bad feeling?"

"I think it might involve Steven."

"You mean Greg."

"Yeah, whatever."

"Have you had any more dreams or visions regarding him?"

"No…"

"Well, I have to agree that this seems unusual. And considering what's happened with Greg Hampton, I don't think it could hurt to put out a flash."

"Flash?"

"You know, like an APB. So the guys on patrol can be on the lookout for her car just in case anything is wrong."

"Do you think something could be wrong?" I ask weakly. "I mean, is it possible that Steven, I mean Greg, is still around? I kind of assumed he'd have hit the road by now."

"We haven't had any luck tracking him down, so I assumed the same thing. I think it's a pretty safe assumption."

"Maybe there's a logical explanation for Mom being gone…"

"I'm sure there is, Samantha. But don't feel bad about calling me. I think, under the circumstances, it was the right thing to do."

"Right…"

"Let me know if she gets home, okay?"

"Yeah. And you'll let me know if you find out anything?"

"Absolutely."

I give Ebony all the details I can think of regarding Mom's car and what she might have been wearing, but the truth is, I never saw her yesterday. After I hang up, I try calling some of her co-workers, but none of them went in to work on Saturday.

"You might try calling Marco Salvador," suggests June Bishop, a bookkeeper. "He would've been there doing the Saturday program yesterday." Then she gives me his number, and I call.

"Sorry to bother you," I tell him, explaining who I am. "I'm trying to find my mom. I think she went in to work yesterday, but she, uh, she hasn't come home."

"I saw her in the office yesterday morning," he says. "Then she left shortly before noon with a guy. I guess she was going to lunch…or calling it a day."

"Do you recall what the guy looked like?" I ask, hearing a tremor in my voice.

"Nice-looking guy," he says. "Well dressed. He looked like a businessman. Maybe thirty-something. Blondish hair."

"Did you happen to notice a car?"

"No. They were in the building when I saw them."

"Okay, thanks…"

"Anything wrong?" he asks with concern.

"I'm not sure."

"Well, let me know if I can be of any more help. Your mom's a great lady, Samantha. I enjoy working with her."

"Yeah…" I swallow against a lump in my throat. "Thanks."

I call Ebony back now. "I think Steven was at the park-district building yesterday," I say quickly, relaying what Marco just told me. "I think Mom left with him."

"In her car?"

"I don't know. Marco didn't see a car. Maybe it was Steven's."

"I'll send someone over to check the parking lot."

"Right…" I feel tears burning my eyes.

"It's going to be okay, Samantha."

"I-I hope so."

"We're on it."

"Right…" I let out a small sob. "But what should I do? Should I go look for her…for them…or…"

"Just stay put. No, on second thought I don't want you home alone right now, Samantha. It might not be safe. Can you go to Olivia's?"

"She and her family are gone for the day…"

"Then do you mind hanging with me?"

"Not at all. Do you mind?"

"Of course not!" Then she gives me directions to her condo, telling me to bring an overnight bag. "Just in case."

"Right."

I leave Mom another note, saying that I'm with Ebony and that I have my phone, and begging her in big, bold, uppercase letters to "PLEASE CALL ME ASAP!" Then I lock up the house and leave. As I drive across town to Ebony's place, I pray. I pray and pray and pray. And I try to be brave, but I feel like I'm about six years old again—and like my world is about to cave in. Or maybe it already has and I just don't know it.

Ebony meets me in the parking lot. She's wearing a brown velour warmup suit and looks like she might've just gotten out of the shower. But she seems glad to see me as she points to where I should park my car. She hugs me when I get out. "We're going to figure this out," she says with confidence that I can't even begin to muster just now. Then she leads me up the stairs to her second-floor condo unit, which overlooks the river.

"This is a really nice place," I say as I gaze out the window, taking in her fantastic view of water and trees. Then I turn around and check out the spacious living area, which is done in rich, warm earth tones—russets and golds and mossy greens. "I like your décor too."

She smiles. "Thanks. Kind of eclectic."

"But totally cool."

She puts a hand on my shoulder now, looking directly into my eyes. "How are you doing, Samantha?"

I suddenly feel close to tears again. "I've been praying a lot, and I'm trying not to freak, but the truth is, I'm so scared for Mom. I know she would've called me by now…if she could."

Ebony nods. "Yes, I'm sure she would've too. Any chance her phone is dead?"

I shrug. "Even if it was, I'm sure she would've found a pay phone."

"And you haven't had any more visions? No new information?"

"No…" I just shake my head. "I wish it was the kind of thing I could control," I admit. "But God doesn't work like that."

"I understand." Then she shows me to her guest room, which is done in peaceful shades of aqua blue and green. "Make yourself at home," she says. "I need to make some more calls and take care of a few things. Then I think you and I should go out and do a little looking around ourselves."

I nod hopefully. "That sounds good."

While Ebony makes her calls, I call Zach's rehab place. But the man on the other end asks me to leave a message. Without going into details, I tell him that it's urgent and that Zach needs to call as soon as he can. Then I call Olivia, filling her in on the latest details and asking her to pray.

"You can count on it, Sam. In fact, as soon as we hang up, I'll call the church's prayer chain and ask them to pray too."

"Thanks."

"Where are you anyway? Not home alone, I hope."

"I'm staying at Ebony's…for now."

"And you know you can stay with me if you want," she offers. "We'll probably be home around dinnertime."

"I'll keep you posted." After I hang up, I consider calling Conrad as well, but then I think of all he has on his mind with little Katie and how he and Alex might be on the road coming home by now, and I decide not to bother him yet.

"I haven't had lunch," Ebony says. "How about you?"

I shrug. "I'm not really hungry."

"Come on," she urges me, "every cop knows that even when you don't feel like it, you need to eat to keep your strength up."

"Is that why I always see patrol cars at Dunkin' Donuts?" I ask, trying to be funny but feeling pathetic.

She chuckles. "Well, I'm not really into donuts, but I was thinking about Rosie's Deli."

I nod. "That actually sounds good."

Ebony uses her unmarked car to drive us downtown. I'm guessing that means we're on official police business now, and that makes me feel better. It also makes me feel better to walk into Rosie's. This used to be my dad's favorite lunch spot. And I can't come here without thinking of him. I try to imagine him, up there in heaven. I wonder if he can see Mom right now…if he knows where she is and what's going on.

After I order my pastrami on rye, which Ebony insists on paying for, I step back and silently pray again. And okay, it's not like I'm praying to my dad—I know that's not how it works— but I think about him as I pray to my heavenly Father. And I am comforted, knowing that they are both up there, both looking out for me—and I believe for my mom too.

"I was just thinking about my dad," I tell Ebony once we're seated.

She nods. "Interestingly…so was I."

"Do you think he knows where Mom is?"

"I don't know." She frowns now. "What is your general feeling about Greg—or Steven, as you think of him? Do you have any sense of what kind of a person he really is?"

"Besides a jerk and a con man?"

"Yes, besides that. Just toss out some general impressions."

"Well, he's really smooth. But not in what I think of as a good way."

"Explain…"

"I sometimes thought he was too good to be real."

"And you were right."

"He treated my mom really well…in a slick, almost patronizing way. I think it made me suspicious that he complimented her so much. Not that Mom isn't smart and pretty and stuff. But he sort of took it too far."

"Disingenuous."

"Yes."

"Did you ever notice him, say, lose his temper? Get angry?"

"Not really. I mean, he got irritated at Zach, especially when he went missing on the ski trip. But then we were all pretty fed up with him."

"What did he say to Zach?"

"Oh, I can't remember exactly. And maybe it wasn't what he said as much as how he said it. I guess he did sound pretty angry."

"But he didn't do anything to Zach?"

"No, he was driving at the time. But he was pretty uptight."

We pause as the girl brings our food. Then Ebony bows her head and says a prayer. It seems to be more about my mom than the food, which is a relief. Then she changes the subject, which is also a relief, since thinking about Steven was starting to make my stomach hurt.

"Does your mom have many friends?" asks Ebony.

"Not really. My parents used to have couples who were friends. But after Dad died, Mom didn't really do much with them. I think it was hard…like she felt weird, like something was missing."

"I can understand."

"Mom hung with Paula a little, before she met Steven, and then he monopolized her time."

"Is that the woman who's a counselor?"

"Yes. But she's not the most sensible person in the world. In fact, when Mom didn't come home last night, I figured she and Paula might be out partying."

"Have you spoken to Paula?"

"No, but I left a message, asking her to call if she'd seen my mom."

"And she hasn't called?"

"Not yet."

"Any other friends?"

"Not that I can think of. I mean, she sometimes does things with co-workers, but I don't think that's the case here."

"No, I don't either. I was just curious. Not as a cop but as a friend."

"A friend?"

"Well, I'd been thinking recently that I haven't really tried to befriend your mom… I wondered if maybe I should."

"She hasn't always been very nice to you," I admit.

"I know she resented me," says Ebony, "for how your dad was killed. And I suppose that made it easy for me to keep a safe distance from her."

"And there wouldn't have been any real reason to be around her," I point out. "It's not like you'd been friends before Dad died."

"No…but then you came along, Samantha." Ebony sort of laughs. "It's so ironic really."

"What?"

"Well, back when your dad and I were partners, that sort of connected me to your mom, to your family, because naturally, he'd talk about you guys. I always felt like I sort of knew you."

"And then it ended."

"Yes. And I was sad to lose that connection."

"And then I showed up."

She smiles. "That was a good day, Samantha."

"For me too."

"So I suppose I thought your mother and I might become friends as a result somehow."

"But she hasn't been overly friendly."

"I think we still have a ways to go."

"But I think, for the most part, she's moved on," I say. "I know she respects you, Ebony."

"I respect her too."

"And she appreciates the help you've given us with Zach. That really means a lot to her."

"But there's still a wall."

"I think she's been jealous of you."

Ebony frowns. "Why?"

"Probably because I admire you…because I want to be a detective like you."

Her eyes light up. "And you're already off to a good start. I'd think your mother would be proud of you."

"She sort of is, but I think she struggles with it…I mean, with my gift. I think that's mainly because she's struggling with God too. She keeps pushing Him away."

"That doesn't help."

"No, and it sort of set her up to be hurt by Steven. I mean, if she'd been walking with God, I'm sure she would've realized that Steven was bad news."

"What makes you so sure?"

"Because I believe God gives all of us intuitions. He sends us little signals, you know, clues as to whether we're making the right choices or not."

"That still, small voice."

"Exactly." I nod as I pick up the other half of my sandwich. "And when you tune out God, you also tune out His guidance and direction."

"And you become like a boat, lost out there on a rough sea, without a rudder to steer yourself home."

I sigh sadly. "That's my mom."

We're just finishing our food when my cell phone rings. I eagerly answer it, hoping it's Mom. But it's Paula.

"I got your message, Sam. What's going on?"

So I quickly explain that Mom's missing, possibly with Steven.

"Are you saying that she's run off with Steven?"

"No, of course not."

"What then?"

"I don't know, but someone at Mom's work thinks Steven might've shown up there yesterday." I try to keep my voice even and calm although a part of me is on the verge of tears again.

"Well, in the last conversation I had with Beth, she was angry at Steven. She wanted to hang that bottom feeder out to dry."

"I know."

Paula asks more questions, and like me, she grows more concerned when I give her the answers. "I can't imagine Beth going willingly with him, Sam."

"I can't either."

"I mean, she sounded a little nutty the other night, acting like we should go out and find him and punish him. But I didn't take her seriously. I just tried to humor her."

"That was probably good." My voice cracks just slightly.

There's a brief pause, and I think maybe I lost my connection, but then she speaks. "So, do you think he's kidnapped her?"

I cringe at that word—I've tried not to go there—I don't want to think it's even possible. "I really...I don't know..."

"Well, if I hear anything, I'll get back to you. You do the same."

"Sure."

"And, Sam?"

"Yeah."

"I'm sorry. I mean, you've been through a whole lot already. And in my opinion, you're holding it together better than anyone else in your family."

"Uh, thanks." I feel a tear slipping down my cheek, and Ebony reaches across the table, pats my hand, and hands me a paper napkin.

"Keep it up, girl."

"I'll try."

After I hang up, I wipe my tears and blow my nose on the napkin, then I fill Ebony in on the details. "So I guess I was wrong about Paula. She's not stupid. She wouldn't have gone out looking for Steven after all."

"*Looking* for Steven?" Ebony looks confused now.

"I overheard Mom talking to Paula about them going out like vigilantes, you know, and making Steven sorry for what he'd done."

"Do you think your mom might've done that on her own?"

"It seems unlikely. I mean, she *did* go to work yesterday morning. Marco saw her there. And then he saw her leave with someone who fits Steven's description. It sounds to me like he came looking for her." I take a quick breath. The more we talk about this, the more pieces we put together, the scarier it feels.

Ebony nods soberly. "Yes, and that reminds me, Samantha. One of the calls I made before we left was to verify whether your mom's car is at the park-district building or not."

"Is it?"

"No."

"Do you think that means they could be in her car?"

"I think it's a possibility. I asked the guys to keep a lookout for Steven's car as well. My guess is that it's somewhere nearby. I also found out he had put the minimum down and made only a few payments, so the car's not even close to being paid off. I'll bet that Steven planned on ditching it. Especially if he suspects we're onto him. He'll know we have the description and license number now, and he'll want to get rid of it, like he's done in the past." Ebony lets out a long sigh.

"So if he's with Mom," I begin carefully, "in her car…what do you think he intends to do with her?" I study Ebony closely, trying to determine if she's as worried as I am.

"That's what I'm trying to figure out." She lays a tip on the table, and we both stand.

"Is that why you wanted to know my impressions of him? You wanted to determine whether or not he's dangerous?"

"Yes."

"Does he have a history of harming anyone? I mean, besides conning people. That's bad enough. But tell me, Ebony—has he ever been violent?"

"There's no record of if. But I'll be honest. We don't know everything about him. There are some gaps. He's used a lot of phony names…it's impossible to track everything. But be assured, we haven't uncovered anything to suggest he's physically harmed anyone."

I let out a deep sigh. I want to feel relieved. I want to believe that Mom's okay. Even so, I can't help but think Steven is up to no good. Especially if he's holding Mom against her will. And isn't that considered kidnapping? And that really seems to be the only explanation. Otherwise she would've called me. I know she would've called. No way would she be gone for twenty-four hours without checking on me, without letting me know what's up. Something is wrong. Very, very wrong. For Ebony's sake, I try to appear brave. But inside I'm having a meltdown. Mom is in danger—I just know it! I feel it deep within me. But besides praying and waiting, what can I do?

Eleven

Ebony cruises around town, occasionally taking a radio call, occasionally talking on her cell. But so far no one has uncovered a thing. Not even Steven's car, which makes me feel slightly hopeful. Is it possible they're not together after all? But then if they're not together, where is Mom? Why hasn't she called? We even stop by the house just to see if it looks like she's been home. But everything is exactly the same, and there are no messages from Mom on the landline.

"Anything here that you need?" Ebony asks as we head for the front door.

I look around at what seems a strangely empty house. I mean, all the furniture and things are still here, and it looks pretty much the same as always. But it feels like the people have all abandoned it. Or maybe they've simply abandoned me.

"No," I tell Ebony. "Nothing here that I need." But what I don't admit is that I need my mom. I need my brother. I need my family. There's a deep ache inside me now, a frightening feeling that nothing is ever going to be right again, like it's all spinning out of control. And I can barely hold back the tears.

"It seems futile to keep driving around," Ebony says as we get back in her car. "Maybe we should take a break...wait for someone to call."

I nod. "Yeah...probably so."

So she drives us back to her condo, and without speaking much, we go off to our separate spaces. She goes to her room, and I go to the guest room, where I lie down on the bed and just cry. And when I'm done crying, I pray.

Dear God, I plead, *please keep Mom safe. Please get her safely home. And although I'm not trying to make a deal with You, I promise to be a much better daughter from now on. I promise that when Mom gets back, I will love her just as she is, God. I'm so sorry I tried to make her into something that she's not ready to become yet. I know Your timing is perfect, God. I trust You to work things out with Mom. And I promise to simply love her. Help me to love her the way You do, God—unconditionally. Amen.* And then I drift into a restless sleep.

The sun makes the car hot...and me sleepy. I am so groggy...as if I've been drugged. I just need some rest. My eyes feel as if someone taped lead weights to them... I can no longer keep them open. But I try to focus on the faded yellow lines going down the center of the road. I try to aim the car to the right of them. I have no idea how fast I'm driving. I don't think I care anymore. What difference does it make?

I've lost track of the mileage numbers. I can't even remember the last sign I saw. Was it Albuquerque? And how long ago was that? I tried to maintain my bearings earlier on, hoping for an opportunity to escape this madman. At one point I actually had it all planned out. Now I'm so tired I can't even remember what the plan was…or why I'm here.

I glance over to the passenger seat now, hoping against hope that maybe he's fallen asleep, that maybe I can pull over and grab my purse from the backseat and jump out and run. But he's wide awake. Studying the map. The gun still in his hand. I glance out at the terrain now. Where would I run to anyway? It's so barren, with nothing but rocks and sagebrush and hills and brown dust. No place to hide.

I notice a sign ahead, and I slow down as I try to focus my eyes to read the words. Like so many of the other signs, it seems to be in Spanish. *Las Cruces 28 miles.* I wonder what that means. Is it a town? Are we in Mexico? And then I no longer care.

"Pull over!" Steven says suddenly.

"What?" I turn and look at him. "There's nothing out here."

He sort of laughs as he tosses the map to the floor of my car, but then he turns serious as he waves the handgun close to my face. "That's the point, Beth. Pull over."

So I pull over to the side of the road, but I don't turn off the car. I just sit there and ponder my fate. With startling clarity, almost as if someone just threw a bucket of cold water over my head, I know exactly what he's going to do next. First, he'll make me get out of the car. Then he'll tell me to walk a ways out, maybe a hundred feet or more, but far enough from the road that a passerby won't spot me.

Not that there are any other cars on this desolate stretch of road. I can't even remember when I last saw a car. Finally, after I'm far enough out, he'll shoot me, probably in the back…maybe the head. And I will fall into the sun-baked dust, and he will leave me there for the vultures and coyotes to pick my bones clean. Perhaps I deserve this sort of ending. Perhaps it's my own fault for being so unbelievably stupid. But what about my children? My kids. Samantha…Zachery…I am so sorry. So, so sorry…

I sit up and gasp for breath, disoriented and confused, and look around to see where I am. But instead of the scorched desert highway, I find myself in a cool, comfortable room with soothing ocean colors. I realize I am safe in Ebony's guest room. But the dream I had was painfully real—and frightening. I leap out of bed and run down the hallway. "I know where Mom is!" I scream. "Ebony! Ebony! I had a dream!"

Tears are streaming down my cheeks when she finds me in the living room. I'm just standing in the center of the room, having what feels like a complete meltdown. I'm shaking and crying, and it feels like I'm going to be sick to my stomach or maybe pass out.

"Sit down," Ebony commands me, leading me to the couch where she eases me down. "Put your head between your knees, Sam. Take some slow, deep breaths." She gently pats my back. "Now just try to relax. Breathe deeply, and when you're ready, you can tell me about your dream."

I do as she says, praying as I take shallow breaths at first and finally deeper ones. I'm surprised to find that I'm not praying in my head, like I often do, but I'm praying out loud. And then I realize that Ebony is praying too. We both pray for Mom, and eventually I feel calm enough to describe my dream. Ebony's ready with a tablet and pen, taking careful notes as I try to remember every single detail.

"Is Albuquerque in Arizona?" I ask when I think I'm about finished.

"New Mexico."

"And the sign—*Las Cruces.* What is that?"

"A town by the Mexican border. Las Cruces means the crosses."

"Oh…" I nod, trying to absorb this.

"I'm calling the FBI." Ebony is already dialing the numbers. I try to listen to her, but my mind is still racing, still trying to determine if I missed some small but important detail. Is there more to my dream than I can consciously recall?

I can hear her relaying the information I just gave her. "No, I don't know which highway it is," she says for the second time, as if trying to make herself clear. She glances at her notes again. "But as I said, there is a sign that says 'Las Cruces 28 miles.'" She pauses. "No, I don't know which direction that would be." She tosses a questioning look at me, and I try to remember.

"The sun was shining in through the passenger's side window," I say quickly.

Her brow creases as she considers this. "South," she states. "We think Las Cruces was twenty-eight miles *south* of the site that we want checked. And keep in mind, we're talking about a very desolate road. Not a major highway. There wouldn't be much traffic." She pauses again. "Yes, definitely. Yes, we'll be right here." Then she hangs up.

"Are they looking for her now?" I ask desperately.

"The FBI is on top of it. Sounds like they'll be sending out state troopers immediately. Naturally, they're not sure which road it is, and the dispatcher said it might be helpful if they can call back to ask you for more details. Are you comfortable with that, Samantha?"

"Of course." I rack my brain to remember more. "There were yellow lines in the center of the highway, pretty faded. And I think there were some potholes, like it wasn't a well-maintained road."

Ebony is furiously writing this down. "This is good, Samantha. It'll be helpful. Keep going if you can."

"The low hills were to the right of the road. It seemed more flat on the left side."

"That sounds like the hills were to the west then, if the car was going south like we're assuming."

"Yes, based on the sun's direction, that would be right. But that's only if I was in the same time zone…you know in the dream. Like real time. But suppose what I saw happened hours ago? What if it was morning and the sun was on the east side? They'd be going north."

"Considering how far away Las Cruces is and how long they must've been driving, it seems unlikely they'd have been there in the morning. And even if that was somehow the case, why would they be driving north if Greg is trying to get away?"

"Mom seemed exhausted. I think she'd done all the driving."

"Poor Beth." Ebony shook her head. "For now, let's assume that your dream was in real time."

I nod. "It did seem more like afternoon than morning. Something about the light…or the heat…I'm not even sure."

"How about the road when you—I mean, your mom— pulled over? How did it look right there?"

"There was hardly any shoulder on the road, just dirt, and it sort of dropped down, like a foot or so. The car couldn't get completely off the highway, but there wasn't traffic, so it wouldn't be a problem."

"How about the gun, Samantha? Do you remember what it looked like?"

"Not very big and dark colored. It almost seemed like a toy gun, but I suspect it was real."

"I'll show you some photos," she says. "Maybe you can pick it out. It will be important to identify the weapon." She stands and goes to her bookcase.

"You mean if Mom's been shot?"

She turns and looks at me with concerned eyes. "To iden-tify Greg, or Steven. He got that gun somewhere. It will be part of his trail." She returns with a gun book, and after a few min-utes I find one that seems similar.

"That's a Glock," she says with uncertainty. "Are you sure?"

"I'm not positive, but it looks like it."

"That's a serious gun."

"What gun isn't serious?"

"Good point. How about Greg—or Steven? What was he wearing? Do you recall?"

I struggle to remember. "Dark pants, like they were proba-bly suit pants. Not black, but maybe charcoal gray. And a light blue shirt that was partially buttoned and not tucked in. Kind of sloppy looking, but it seemed like a dress shirt, like he'd been dressed for a business meeting."

She's writing this down. "And your mom… Do you recall what she had on?"

I try to remember. "Blue jeans…but I'm not sure which top. Although I think it had short sleeves…because her forearms were bare. And I could see her watch—the silver one that's like a bracelet."

"Did you see what time it was?"

I close my eyes and strain my brain to remember. I definitely recall seeing the watch's face, but where were the hands pointing? "On the right side of the dial," I say suddenly. I look up at the clock in Ebony's kitchen. "Like two fifteen…or three fifteen."

"And it's nearly five now," Ebony says. "And even though they're an hour ahead, let's assume it was before four our time when they stopped."

"Do you think she's okay?"

Just then the phone rings, and Ebony answers and immediately tells whoever is on the other end the new information I just gave her. I'm relieved I don't have to talk to anyone else just yet. I bow my head and pray some more. I try not to remember the chill of my mother's fear…or her prediction of what Steven was about to do.

When Ebony hangs up, I ask if they've found the road.

"Not yet. Apparently there are a number of roads in that area. They're trying to narrow it down and will soon have a helicopter out looking."

"Would it help if we went down there," I say suddenly, "like we did with Kayla in Arizona?"

"I'm hoping they'll find her much sooner than that," says Ebony in a serious tone. "The best bet is for them to get there…and get there fast."

"I know…" I choke back a sob. "I just can't stand this…this waiting and not knowing. Why does God show me these things when there's absolutely nothing I can do about it?"

"Oh, Samantha." She sits beside me and puts an arm around me. "You are not doing *absolutely nothing.* What we've just given the FBI is a really big something. It's enough for them to find your mom—and to arrest him."

"But this waiting…"

"Let's just pray, Samantha. That's really all we can do now."

And so we pray. We take turns, but Ebony prays the most. And her words wash over me like a smooth, cool blanket of comfort, and just as I'm beginning to feel hopeful that Mom will be found alive and okay, my phone rings.

I quickly answer, hoping beyond hope that it will be Mom's voice on the other end, but it's my brother. "Oh, Zach!"

"What's up, Sam? Is something wrong?"

So I tell him the whole ugly story of how Mom is missing, how Steven is involved, and finally my vision in New Mexico, although I leave out the part about the gun. Somehow I don't think Zach needs to hear that just yet. I don't want to upset him too much.

"So what's next?" he demands. "How do we help her?"

I explain that they're already looking for her. "I'm at Ebony's now. I'll stay with her until Mom gets home." Even as I say this, I feel my faith shrinking slightly. What if she never comes home? Still, I need to be strong—for Zach's sake.

"So you think she's okay?" I hear the fear in my brother's voice.

"Oh, sure," I say, trying to sound light and easy. "I think Steven just wanted a quick ride out of town, and he decided that Mom's car would make a good shuttle service. He wouldn't hurt her."

"Poor Mom."

"Yeah…"

We talk awhile longer, and I try to reassure him. Zach already has a lot on his plate… As much as I want to tell him everything, I don't want to give him any reason to mess up his rehab time. I know Mom wouldn't want that either.

"Well, keep me posted," he says. "I'll let them know that you'll be calling here and that it's a family emergency."

"Give them Ebony's name and number if they need verification."

"Okay."

"And remember, Zach," I finally say, "the best thing we can do right now is to pray."

"I'll definitely be doing that."

"I love you, Zach."

"I love you too, Sam. And"—his voice cracks—"I want to be a better brother to you. And a better son to Mom too. This time I'm gonna do it right. You guys will see. We'll be a family again. With God's help, I promise, we will."

I try to hold on to that promise as we say good-bye and hang up. We're going to be a family again. Mom and Zach and me. A family. With God's help…we will.

But as the minutes slowly tick by, doubts creep in. I try to keep praying, and then, to distract ourselves, Ebony and I make chili. It was her mom's recipe, and as she talks about her mom and what a great cook she was, all I can think about is my own mom. She might not be the best cook, but I love her. Will I ever see her again?

bony and I are both fairly quiet during dinner. At times like this, there is only so much small talk a person can make. Fortunately, Ebony seems to understand this. I try to act like I'm enjoying the homemade chili, but the truth is, my stomach feels like I've already swallowed a brick. We're just cleaning up the dinner things when Olivia calls me on my cell phone. I quickly tell her the latest news.

"Oh, Sam," she exclaims. "I'm so sorry. That's horrible. You must be totally freaking."

"Yeah, pretty much." I glance at the clock. It's nearly six thirty now, and we haven't heard anything for close to an hour. "And maybe I should keep my phone line clear," I say suddenly. "In case Mom tries to call me."

"Definitely. I'll be praying, Sam. Keep me posted."

After I hang up, I turn to Ebony. "Do you think it would hurt to call the FBI again? Just in case...I mean, maybe they found her but forgot to call us."

"I don't think it'd hurt anything," she says, reaching for her phone.

Barely breathing, I listen as Ebony makes an inquiry. "But you think maybe you've located the road?" She pauses. "Yes, that sounds right. A search party? Good. What time does the sun set down there? Oh..." She nods as if processing this. "Please let us know as soon as you find out anything... Yes. We appreciate it." Then she hangs up.

"What?" I demand.

"They think they located the road, and they found a sign that fits your description."

"And?"

"They sent out a search party to comb that area just beyond the Las Cruces road sign you saw. They hope to find her before dark."

"When does it get dark in New Mexico?"

She frowns. "They say the sun sets around 6:45 this time of year."

"That's in minutes!"

"Actually, it was an hour ago. Remember, New Mexico is a different time zone. It's 7:40 right now."

"Did they quit looking when it got dark?"

"I don't know. But it probably didn't get dark right when the sun set. I'm sure there was at least an hour of dusk... maybe more."

"I wish I could go down there."

"I know you do, Samantha. But by the time we got a flight, if we could even get one tonight, and by the time we got down there, probably not until morning, your mom could be on her way home."

"I hope you're right..."

"We just need to be patient...and keep praying."

"I know." I look out the window, out over the river where I can still see the sun through the trees. "It looks like the sun won't be going down here for a while," I point out. "Why does it set so early in New Mexico?"

"Remember, living up here in the north, we get more daylight hours this time of year."

"Oh…"

I think this has been the longest day of my life. By eight o'clock, I am frantic. I beg Ebony to call again. "Just see if they have an update."

She agrees, and I listen as she grills them. I can't detect a thing from her vague responses. Still, she doesn't seem pleased with what she finds out. Her forehead is deeply creased by the time she hangs up the phone.

"What?" I demand impatiently.

"The good news is that the search is continuing after dark."

"Is there bad news?"

"They feel certain they've located the site…and they've collected some evidence."

"Evidence?"

She nods, putting a hand on my shoulder. "A shell casing…"

"From the Glock?"

"Most likely."

I take in a sharp breath. "Anything else?"

"And some blood."

Tears are coming now. "My mom's blood?"

"They can't be sure."

"But where is she?"

"They don't know, but right now someone is on the way with dogs…to track her. If she's out there, they should find her very soon."

I sink into a chair by the window and attempt to assimilate this information. My mother has possibly been shot. She's out in the desert. Dogs will be tracking her. "What about Steven?" I ask. "And the car?"

"They think he's made it into Mexico. But all the local authorities have been notified down there. Hopefully someone will pick him up soon."

I feel like I hate that man, like I could kill him if I needed to. But I know that's not a Christian attitude. Still, I'm not sure I care.

"How could they find blood," I persist, "but not find Mom?"

Ebony nods. "I was wondering the same thing. My first guess is that she's been wounded, but not too badly, and that she was able to get away...or..." Then she stops.

"Or what?"

"Or...maybe he forced her back into the car."

"Why would he do that?"

"I'm not sure... To be honest, it wouldn't make much sense. But it doesn't make sense that the searchers wouldn't have found her either. If that was her blood."

"Maybe it's Steven's blood," I say hopefully. "Maybe Mom got the gun from him, shot him, and drove off."

Ebony nods, but I can tell by her eyes she believes this is hopeful thinking on my part. "Maybe... Time will tell."

And so my long night continues. I tell Ebony there's no way I'll be able to go to sleep until I know Mom's okay. She understands.

By ten o'clock my hopes are dwindling fast. "Go ahead and go to bed," I tell Ebony. "I know you have to work tomorrow."

She simply shakes her head. "Not a chance. I am not going to bed until we hear something."

"Do you think that no news is bad news?"

"I'm not sure what to think."

Just then the phone rings, and my heart jolts. I stand by Ebony as she answers it. My pulse is pounding in my ears, and I am so afraid that I can barely breathe. It's like someone has wrapped ice-cold hands around my neck and is squeezing tightly.

"Samantha," says Ebony with brightly shining eyes as she hands me the phone, "it's your mother!"

I feel slightly faint as I reach for the phone. "Mom?" I cry. "Is it really you?"

"Yes, Samantha, it's me." Her voice sounds hoarse and very tired.

"Are you okay?"

"I am now, sweetie. I am now."

Tears stream down my cheeks again. "I'm so glad you're okay, Mom. I've been so freaked. I've been praying and praying."

"And I heard…you're the reason they found me."

"They told you that?"

"Not all the details, just something about a girl in Oregon, a girl who had a dream. They don't even know you're my daughter."

"I love you, Mom! I don't know what I'd do without you. Are you really okay?"

"I am."

"Did Steven shoot you?"

"Yes, but fortunately, he's not a very good shot."

"So you're really okay?"

"I am. Right now they're transporting me to a hospital to check me out…but don't worry. I'm in good hands."

"When will you come home?"

"Probably tomorrow. Right now I just need a good night's sleep."

"I know."

"I'm sure you do."

"I told Zach. He's pretty freaked too."

"I'll call him from the hospital."

"Good."

"And I'll call you in the morning, Samantha. Are you at Olivia's?"

"No, I'm with Ebony."

"Good. Thank her for me."

"Yes. Definitely."

"I love you, Samantha."

"I love you too, Mom." Then we hang up, and I'm still crying. I throw my arms around Ebony and hug her tightly. "She's okay. She said Steven was a bad shot. She's just tired. She'll be home tomorrow."

"That's wonderful," Ebony says when I finally let her go.

"And she said to thank you."

Ebony nods. "That's nice."

"I need to call Zach and Olivia," I say suddenly.

"I think I'll go to bed," she says.

"Me too," I say, "as soon as I tell them the good news."

After I finish my phone calls, I get down on my knees and thank God. I know He's the only reason Mom is safe tonight. He gave me the dream. And He helped the searchers locate her. Without God, my mom would probably still be out there. I wonder if she knows that.

I wake to the sound of a phone ringing. But then I hear Ebony's voice, and I realize once again where I am. And why. And I remember that Mom is okay now. And she'll be coming home today. I quickly shower and dress, and when I find Ebony, she is grinning.

"Good news!"

"Yeah?"

"They picked up Steven, a.k.a. Greg Hampton, just outside of Chihuahua, Mexico, early this morning. He still had your mom's car, but it had broken down outside the city limits, and a policeman came along and ran the plates and discovered it was stolen. He's being held in the Chihuahua city jail until the FBI arrives. After that he'll be extradited to the States."

"Cool."

"Very cool." Ebony takes out a carton of eggs. "I don't know about you, but I think this calls for a real breakfast. You game for my famous cheese omelet?"

"Sounds fantastic. I'm starved."

"You've had a rough weekend, Samantha. Do you feel up to going to school this morning? I could probably write you an excuse."

"That's okay." I situate myself on a barstool at her breakfast counter and watch as she cracks eggs into a bowl. "I'm looking forward to going to school."

"Back to a normal routine?"

"Yeah. I know it sounds crazy, but it seems like a long time since I've seen my friends." Then I tell her about Conrad's little sister and his trip to Seattle. "I'm eager to hear how that went too."

"Lots going on in your life." She pours the eggs into a hot buttered pan, and I listen to them sizzle. "I hope it's not too much for you. And we have that prom situation to solve next weekend. Are you still good to go with that?"

"You bet. I'm so glad Mom's okay that I feel totally energized this morning." I let out a happy sigh. "And next weekend sounds like a long way off."

"It'll come quickly," she warns me as she grates cheese onto the eggs.

"I hope this will be it," I say. "Not that I want anyone at Fairmont to get hurt. I just want us to catch the creeps—to put an end to it." I suddenly remember my dream again, the students who'd been shot...dying on the white marble floor. "I don't see why a terrorist has an interest in doing something like that at a prom."

"I've given that a fair amount of thought myself. I've come up with a theory of sorts."

"What?" I listen closely now.

"Well, it's not that different from the original threat. Remember, I read you parts of it?"

"Yes. But it mostly sounded crazy and mean. Kind of senseless and extreme, really."

"I was trying to understand an extremist point of view. A prom might represent all the things about American culture that are abhorred by jihadi or Islamic terrorists. Think about it— things like materialism, immodesty, immorality. That's not to say all kids who go to proms are like that, but it could be a wrong perception someone has put together out of ignorance."

"Yeah, I can see that."

"So perhaps they decided that a prom is a good place to hit us. It's so unexpected. And proms have never been known for having high security. Not like a ball game or other kinds of community events where police and security guards are abundant. Also, the idea of killing innocent young people, well, that's a real attention getter. It would make world news within the hour. And that's just what they want."

"That's so creepy."

She nods. "I'm just glad you're on top of it."

"I don't feel very on top of it," I admit. "But I hope God is."

"I'm sure of it."

Still, I wonder as I drive to Olivia's house to pick her up for school. After attending two proms that fizzled, I feel a little unsure of myself. And yet I saw God do an amazing miracle just yesterday—using my dream to rescue my mom. Really, how can I doubt?

hat is so incredible," Olivia says after I've filled her in on some of the details from last night's phone conversation with my mom. "Did your mom say where she'd been shot?"

"No. Just that it wasn't serious. I can't wait to hear the whole story."

"Does your mom know that Steven's behind bars?"

"I'm guessing she does, but I haven't talked to her yet today. She's supposed to call me when she knows which flight she'll be on."

"You must be excited to see her."

"Totally." I shake my head now. "I think I kind of took her for granted…or worse. Now I realize how much I love her. And I'm not even going to push her to come to church or to be a Christian or anything. I decided that I just need to love her unconditionally. No pressure."

"I guess we should do that to everyone, huh?"

"Yeah. But sometimes it's hard." I'm thinking about Steven (or Greg) now. I don't know if I could possibly love that jerk. Still, I know that God could do it through me. Mostly I just want to work my way through to forgiving him—with God's help, of course. And then I'd like to forget him.

When we get to school, my friends all want to know about my mom. Thanks to the church's prayer chain—and the school's gossip chain—everyone seems to know something about it. After a while I get tired of repeating the story or straightening out the mixed-up details. "No, my mom wasn't kidnapped and transported to Mexico to become a sex slave."

By lunchtime I try to redirect the conversation at our table by asking Conrad about Katie. He's already told me a little, but it was so overshadowed by my story that I feel I've missed out.

"They won't know whether the medicine is working for at least a week," Conrad tells everyone. "But she was in good spirits."

"She was sure glad to see us," Alex says.

"And sad to see us go," adds Conrad.

Just then my phone rings, and when I realize it's Mom, I leave the table to talk to her.

"I'm on my way to the Albuquerque airport," she tells me. "My flight connects through Salt Lake, and I should arrive in Portland at 7:40."

"Are you feeling okay?" I ask.

"Yes. I'm fine, Samantha. I got a good night's sleep, and the hospital staff was very good to me."

"And your gunshot wound?" I ask quietly, not eager for anyone to overhear me since this isn't something I've made public knowledge with anyone but my closest friends.

"It's really just a flesh wound. He clipped me on the left shoulder. It's sore and bruised but not too serious."

"Did you get your purse and phone back?"

"Not yet. But the FBI people have been extremely helpful. They got me some photo ID so I can board the flight and even helped me with the tickets. I didn't want to wait for my purse and things to be returned, assuming that will even happen. I'm just eager to get home."

"I'll pick you up at the airport," I promise. "I guess you won't have any bags. How about if I meet you in front?"

"That sounds perfect, Samantha."

"Be safe."

"You too."

After school I drive to the police station. I'm curious as to whether Ebony has any news, and I want to let her know that Mom is on her way home. I park my car on a side street about a block from the precinct, and I'm just getting out and locking the door when I'm hit with a flash of light. I put my hand on the roof of my car and just close my eyes, bracing myself for whatever God is about to show me.

I can see Brandon, and it's clear that he's really scared—almost as if he's in fear for his life. He's running through an open area, like between two buildings, and several guys are chasing him, yelling threats, saying they're going to kill him. He ducks into a doorway and runs down a hallway and finally ends up in what sort of looks like a locker room, although I don't see any lockers. He jumps into one of those big carts that are for used towels, and for a moment I think he might've escaped the bullies. But they notice the cart move slightly, and they rip back the towels and haul him out. No one else is around to see as they take turns holding him and beating him so badly that his glasses are smashed, and it looks like his nose is broken, and he is bleeding…and sobbing. He begs them for mercy, but they just make fun of him for crying like a baby. And they drop him to the floor, kicking him a few more times before they take off. Brandon lies motionless in a heap on the floor. It's as if he's dead.

I open my eyes and am shaking with fury. Why are those guys acting like that? How can they be so cruel, so hateful, so vicious and mean? And how are they getting away with it? From what I could see, this criminal act occurred on school grounds. Although the locker room seemed empty... Perhaps it was after school hours. Still, doesn't Fairmont High bear some of the responsibility for these criminal actions? Shouldn't they be held accountable if one of their students is being bullied like this?

Feeling righteously indignant for Brandon's sake, I march into the precinct and seek out Ebony.

"Something wrong?" she asks when I blast into her office.

"Brandon," I say simply. "I just had a vision where he was viciously beaten again, nearly to death."

She nods with a frown. "Any idea about when, where, how?"

"Well, it seemed to take place in a locker room. Now if he really goes to Fairmont, like he told me, shouldn't the school protect him?"

"Yes. Good point. Let's do a little research, get our facts straight, and then I'll give them a call. For starters, I want you to verify that Brandon is a student there. Get his full name for me, and I'll try to find out if he's reported any violence."

So I spend the afternoon perusing the Fairmont High annual. But I don't see anyone who resembles Brandon. And the kids I find who are named Brandon are not him. I also look for guys named Allen since that was a name I'd heard in a vision before. But there's only one Allen, and he doesn't look anything like the kid I met in the arcade last weekend. Then I decide to look through some of the other high school annuals. We have quite a stack. And in my third one—the same yearbook I looked through last week for the McKinley prom— I find a kid named Brandon Allen, who looks just like my Brandon. According to the yearbook, which is for last year, Brandon was a sophomore there. So he'd be a junior now. I wonder why he told me he went to Fairmont if he really goes to McKinley.

I take the yearbook to Ebony, who's on the phone having what sounds like a serious conversation. Not wanting to disturb her, I stick a Post-it by the photo, make an arrow pointing at him, and write "this is the kid." Then I leave Ebony to her phone call.

After that, I go through the Fairmont yearbook again, more carefully this time, hoping to find the girl in the pale green dress. But the truth is, so much has happened since I had the dream that her face has gotten pretty blurry in my memory. Still, I put Post-its next to photos of several girls who seem like possibilities. I definitely think the Fairmont students have more of that rich-kid image that I remember from my dream. I also make note of the girls' names, thinking I will look them up when I stop by their school at the end of the week.

By the time I'm ready to leave the precinct, I feel I've made real progress. I also feel seriously tired.

"I checked with McKinley High," Ebony tells me when I stop by her office to say good-bye. "Brandon Allen was a student there last year. But he transferred out last spring."

"Did they say where?"

She nods. "Fairmont."

"So he wasn't lying. Did they say why he transferred?"

"They weren't exactly forthcoming, but when I pushed, they did suggest he'd had some social difficulties."

"That's a strange way to describe bullying."

"I don't think any administrators want to admit that their school has bullying going on. Although I did offer to send them some information for creating an antibullying policy, and they actually seemed interested."

"That's something."

"The counselor did say that Brandon is an underachiever."

"What does that mean exactly?"

"She said he has a genius IQ but performs poorly in class."

"I'd do poorly in class too," I say, "if I spent half my time running for my life."

"Yes, I suggested as much. But according to her, he never lodged a complaint against the bullies."

"You can't really blame him for that. What happens when the bullies find out that you tattled? They turn up the heat."

"Yes. It's a gnarly problem."

"So what should I do next?" I ask.

"Well, it's too late for me to reach anyone at Fairmont, but I plan to find out what's going on there. I'll also check out his home situation and try to make sure he's not at serious risk. Having his full name makes this all much easier, Samantha. Good work on finding it."

"I might be getting warmer with the prom girl too," I say. "I found some possibilities, and I'm looking forward to going to Fairmont on Friday."

"Do you have any inclinations," Ebony begins carefully, "as to whether or not Brandon might be connected to your visions about the prom?"

"What do you mean?"

"I mean that sometimes victims can retaliate." Ebony looks evenly at me.

"Retaliate?" I frown. "I don't think he's like that. In every vision I've had, he doesn't even fight back. He actually seems very nonviolent. He's the victim, Ebony. He needs our help."

"I agree." She nods. "But I just wanted to know if you suspected anything else, Samantha. No stone unturned, you know."

"I know. But I really think God just wants us to help him. And maybe when I go to Fairmont, I can talk to him again."

"Yes. That would be good. And maybe we'll have more information on him by then."

"Great. It'll be such a relief to know that he's safe. That last vision—the beating—it was so severe it made me feel sick."

"I understand." Ebony frowns as she writes something down.

"Well, I'll let you get back to work," I say, heading to the door.

"I'm so glad your mom's on her way home." Ebony brightens now. "When does she get in?"

So I tell her when I'm picking Mom up. "By the way, will she get her car back?"

"Yes. The FBI will pick it up and go over it for evidence first."

"And hopefully her purse and things will still be there."

"Hopefully."

"Do you think there's any chance she'll get her money back? I mean, what he stole from her bank account?"

"According to what the FBI told me, Greg had quite a bit of cash stashed away in a bank down there. It seems he was in the process of buying an oceanfront home where he planned to live the good life."

"What a selfish jerk."

"Dirty, rotten scoundrel."

"I know that as a Christian I'm supposed to forgive him," I say quietly. "But I think it's going to be tough."

"God's strength is made perfect in our weakness."

"Good thing. Because I feel pretty weak about forgiving him right now."

"You can only do what you can do, Samantha. Ask God to help you with the rest of it." She smiles. "I'm not worried about you. Somehow you always manage to do the right thing."

"Thanks to God's help," I point out.

"Well, don't think about it too hard. Just enjoy having your mom back. And remember, she's been through quite an ordeal. She may need some TLC."

"That's not a problem. In fact, I want to go home and make sure it's shipshape before I pick her up."

"Your mom is a lucky—no, I mean *blessed* woman."

I have to laugh. "Considering all the things she's been through, I don't think I'd describe her life quite like that."

"No," Ebony says, "I didn't expect you would."

But as I leave, I sort of figure out what Ebony meant. She was just trying to give me an offhanded compliment. And I do appreciate that. Just the same, I don't think my mom's been overly lucky or blessed. If anything, her life seems to have been somewhat cursed. Okay, that's a little harsh. But when you consider that her husband was murdered, her son became a drug addict and nearly went to prison, and most recently she was literally kidnapped and shot... Lucky and blessed? I'm not feeling it.

Fourteen

On the way home from the precinct, I stop to pick up some fresh flowers for my mom. Then I spend a couple of hours cleaning and straightening our house. Not that it was bad, but I want it to be very welcoming. Finally it's nearly seven, and I head out to the airport. I cannot wait to see Mom.

Naturally, traffic is heavier than I expected, so instead of getting there before her flight lands, I find her waiting outside the terminal and looking very tired. She's wearing a baggy blue warmup suit, one I've never seen before, and there's a rainbow-striped carry-on bag next to her feet, which are shod in bright orange rubber flip-flops. I don't think I've ever seen my mom in flip-flops. This is interesting. I pull up, jump out, and run over and gently hug her, trying not to bump her wounded shoulder.

"Oh, Samantha," she says with tears in her eyes, "it's so good to see you."

"It's fantastic to see you, Mom. Here, let me get that bag for you." I pick up her funky striped bag and toss it into the backseat. "Where did you get this anyway?"

She sort of laughs. "The hospital folks and FBI were generous. When I arrived last night, I didn't have much of anything.

They provided me with these sweats and some other things to help get me on my way."

"How's your shoulder?" I ask as I open the passenger door and help her inside.

"It aches." She groans as she reaches for the seat belt. "I should've taken some Advil at the end of the flight, but I thought I'd wait until I got home and take some pain meds the doctor prescribed. I was afraid they might knock me out and I'd get lost in the terminal and never find you."

"Go ahead and take one now if you want. I can get you safely home."

"They're in that wild-looking bag."

So I get her bag, and we fish out the prescription. I hand her my bottle of water, she takes a couple of pills, and we're on our way.

"Yes, this is a rather unique outfit," she says as I drive away from the terminal. "But last night when they brought me to the hospital, I was a mess. My shirt was soaked in blood…so were my jeans. Plus they were filthy. I had no shoes—"

"No shoes?"

"He made me take them off."

"Why?"

"To keep me from running, I think."

"Oh…"

She leaned back into the seat and sighed. "It's been a long couple of days."

"I can imagine… Why don't you just relax, Mom?"

So she does. And despite my burning curiosity to hear all the details of her recent misadventure, I simply drive and hope that her pain pills are working.

"We're home already?" she says happily as I turn off the car.

"Yep." I grab her bag, then run around and help her out of the car.

"Thanks, Samantha. But I'm really not an invalid. I can walk."

"I know, but your pain meds…" I link my arm with hers and guide her into the house. "Besides, you might as well enjoy a little pampering when you can get it."

She nods as I unlock the front door. "Yes. Good thinking."

"Home sweet home," I say as I flick on a light. "Are you hungry?"

"Just thirsty. I ate on the plane."

"Soda?" I offer as we go into the kitchen where I've placed the floral arrangement in her favorite crystal vase in the center of the island.

"Oh, everything looks so lovely, Samantha." She sits on a barstool, then leans over to smell the blooms. "And fresh flowers too!"

I get a glass, put in ice, fill it with her favorite—natural raspberry soda—then set it in front of her.

"Perfect." She takes a sip and sighs. "Oh, it is so good to be home."

"And I know you're tired," I say. "And although I'm full of questions, I'll wait until tomorrow before I start grilling you."

She smiles, kind of sadly. "I appreciate that, Samantha. And don't worry, I want to tell you the whole story. But I am tired."

"You're not going to work tomorrow, are you?"

"Probably not. I'm supposed to go see my regular doc-tor…for my shoulder. I already let the office know I had an accident, but I'll call in tomorrow to see if anything is pressing."

"An accident? Is that what you call it?"

"I just couldn't bring myself to admit that I'd been kid-napped and shot by my ex-boyfriend, the con man." She looks at me with weary eyes. "Do you think I'm terribly silly and shallow?"

"No, not at all. I don't blame you. Not everyone needs to know all the details of your life."

"My thinking exactly." Her eyelids seem to be drooping now.

"Maybe we should get you to your room," I suggest. "It looks like those pain pills are really kicking in."

She nods sleepily. "Yes. I think you may be right."

So I walk with her upstairs. I help her out of her sweat jacket and into an easy-to-get-on pajama top. Then I make sure she has a glass of water by her bed and her pain pills handy, although I remind her that she shouldn't have another one until after two in the morning.

"Two," she repeats after me groggily. "I'll try to remember that."

"Here," I say, reaching for a notepad on her dresser. "I'll write it down for you."

"Thank you, Nurse Samantha." She gives me a goofy grin now. "By the way, you're much prettier than last night's nurse."

"Thanks," I say. "I take after my mom."

Then I help her into bed and tell her to sleep well. By the time I turn off the light, I think she's already drifting off. Poor Mom.

The next morning I get up early. My plan is to dress for school and then fix Mom some breakfast, which I'll take to her in bed. But I find her already up. She's downstairs in the kitchen making coffee. She has that funky blue sweat jacket over her pajamas, but she's actually humming to herself as she measures the coffee.

"How are you feeling?" I ask.

She turns and smiles. "Pretty good actually."

"Because I was thinking I could stay home if you—"

"No no…" She shakes her head. "I don't want you missing school for me, Samantha. I'm fine. In fact, my shoulder seems much better."

"But you'll still see your doctor?"

"Sure. I don't think there's much to be done for it. It really is only a flesh wound. The bullet just skimmed over the top of my shoulder."

"That was lucky."

She nods. "Or maybe God was watching over me."

"Well, people were praying for you."

"I could tell."

I consider this as I watch her filling the carafe with water. Is she just humoring me…or is there something more?

"I have a lot to tell you, Samantha."

"I have more than an hour before I need to go to school," I point out as I fill a bowl with Raisin Bran.

So while we sit at the island, eating cereal and drinking coffee, Mom tells me what happened.

"It was partially my fault," she begins. "I'd been calling Steven all week, leaving messages. I hadn't said anything specific, just that I needed to speak to him…that it was urgent. I think I was hoping I'd be able to talk him into giving me back the money he'd stolen. I thought I could reason with him."

"Oh…"

"Yes. You're probably thinking I was being stupid. I thought I was being brave and smart. Finally I got hold of him on Saturday morning. I called him from my office, and he actually answered. So I told him that I'd been the victim of some kind of credit-card fraud and that I needed his help to sort it out." She shakes her head. "I told him that he was the only one I could trust, that I'd emptied another savings account, and that I was walking around with this big pile of cash, and I wanted to put it someplace safe."

"You told him *that*?"

"Stupid, I know." She sighs. "It was the best I could think of—a way to lure him in. My plan was to confront him, to make him return my money or I would call the cops. I asked him to meet me at work. Even though it was a Saturday, there were a few people around. It seemed safer than being alone at home. But I never expected him to show up with a gun."

"He brought the gun to your office?"

She nods. "He asked me where my stash of cash was, and I told him it was in my purse, which he immediately confiscated. Then, with the gun hidden beneath his jacket, he *escorted* me to my car."

"Why did you go with him?" I demand. "Don't you know that's the worst thing to do? You're always supposed to run, Mom. Once they have you in the car, your odds of escaping go way down."

"That occurred to me, Samantha. But seeing that gun… knowing we had kids in the building… Well, I just didn't want anyone to get hurt."

"What about you?"

"I honestly didn't think Steven would use it on me. And he actually told me that the gun was simply his means to protect us, in case someone tried to steal my money on the way to the car."

"And you believed that?"

"Not completely. Part of me was saying, *run for it!* Another part of me thought I could control this. That I could make him see my point of view and force him to do the right thing." She takes a sip of coffee. "Steven had on a nice business suit, and he was actually being sort of polite, almost charming as we went downstairs. But when we got to the car and he saw there was no pile of money in my purse, he was mad. He figured out that I was trying to trap him and that I knew he'd stolen my money. He told me to start driving."

"And you did."

"Yes. First we stopped at his car, which was parked a few blocks away, almost like he'd suspected something was up. He made me get out, and with the gun at my back, he made me unload some bags and put them into the back of my car. Then we filled up my tank with gas, and he pulled out a map and told me to drive east."

"East?"

"Yes. We drove to the other side of Oregon and into Idaho before he told me to start driving south. I had no idea where we were going. But he just sat there in the passenger seat with his gun and his map, and I couldn't really argue with him. I tried and tried to reason with him. But he finally told me to shut up. He made it clear that he could easily get rid of me. Much of the terrain we passed through was desolate, and as he continually pointed out, there were lots of good places to dump a body."

"Oh, Mom…" I shake my head. "How terrifying."

"Yes. But I still thought I was going to get away. Until he made another phone call… It was after midnight by then. I don't even know where we were. But he called someone as if to verify that the person was at the right address."

"Huh?" Mom is losing me now.

"Our address, Samantha. Steven told me that he had a man parked outside our house, ready to break in and get you if I gave him any problem."

"He said that?"

"At first I told him I didn't believe him, but then he dared me to call his bluff… I didn't think I could do that. By then I knew I was dealing with a madman. I started remembering other nice-looking, charming men who turned out to be sociopaths. Guys like Ted Bundy and Scott Peterson. They look good on the outside but underneath are the devil. That's when I started getting truly scared."

"What about when you needed to use a bathroom," I suggest, thinking of all the ways I would have tried to escape, "or when you had to stop for gas? Couldn't you have made a run for it?"

"Not with the threat of his buddy breaking into our house, Samantha. Not with you alone and not knowing what was up." She peers at me. "Did you know what was going on yet? On Saturday night?"

"I was a little worried," I admit. "But I got home late from the prom-surveillance thing, and I just figured you were out with

Paula and would be home before long. I didn't realize you hadn't come home until morning. Sorry…"

"It wasn't your responsibility, Samantha. I'm the parent, remember."

"Yeah."

"Anyway, my bathroom breaks were either in roadside rest areas where Steven accompanied me to the door and waited, or desolate stretches where I had to use a bush outside the car. But after a while, I was so dehydrated I didn't even need to go."

"Poor Mom." I refill her coffee cup.

"Yes. That's one thing they immediately treated me for at the hospital. I can't even remember how many IVs they used on me."

"So how long did you drive?"

"I lost track, but more than twenty-four hours. Naturally, Steven didn't want to use the major freeways, didn't want to be spotted. I'm sure he thought someone would be looking for us by then. We took lots of back roads, lots and lots of back roads, and New Mexico is a long way from Oregon." Mom gets a kind of lost expression now, like she's still on the road and thinking she'll never get home.

"So you saw the sign to Las Cruces," I say, hoping to hurry things along. "Twenty-eight miles…and that's when he tells you to pull over."

Mom blinks. "How did you know that?" Then she nods knowingly. "Oh, yes…the girl up in Oregon who had a vision and called the FBI."

"Actually, it was a dream, and Ebony called the FBI."

She sort of smiles. "Thank God for both of you."

"So you were afraid," I continue. "You thought this was the end, Steven was going to shoot you, you would fall facedown in the dust, and the coyotes and vultures would pick your bones clean."

Mom looks stunned now. "You got that too? In the dream?"

"God's amazing, Mom."

"I know…"

"So…Steven told you to get out of the car?"

"Yes. I knew by then that he planned to go to Mexico. He had someone already down there…a woman…probably his next victim. It was late in the day; it would soon be dark, no traffic. It was time to get rid of me. I'd been useful as a driver, and my car came in handy since he'd hoped it was less recognizable than his. So he told me to take off my shoes and get out. At first I stayed in the car, and I pleaded with him to let me keep my shoes—and even to give me my purse and cell phone. I told him that I would wait, giving him plenty of time to get across the border before I called for help. I even promised that I wouldn't turn him in at all. He didn't believe me."

"No, of course not."

"I asked him about you then, if you would be okay if I cooperated with him. And he said yes—as long as I cooperated. For a moment I thought he wasn't really going to shoot me. I thought he was just going to ditch me. No shoes. No phone. No money. I'd probably be stuck out there all night…and he'd be long gone. Why not? Then he reached over and took the keys out of the ignition and told me to get out. That's when I saw something cold and evil in his eyes, and that's when I knew…"

"That he was going to shoot you?"

She nods sadly. "I knew."

"So what did you do?"

"Very, very slowly I took off my shoes. I was trying to think of something, anything to stop this…and I even prayed, Samantha. I begged God to protect you, to keep you and Zach safe. And then I got out of the car and walked around to the other side where Steven was out and waiting for me. And just then I noticed a vehicle coming toward us. A yellow pickup, quite a ways down the road, but rolling along just the same. Steven saw me looking, and he turned and looked too." Mom pauses as if to catch her breath, and it's all I can do not to say, "Hurry up! Finish the story!" But I wait as she takes a sip of coffee.

"The minute Steven turned his head to look at the truck, I took off running," she says. "And even though I was barefoot, I ran as fast as my feet would take me. I heard him yell 'Stop!' but I just kept going. I don't know how far off the road I was when I heard the gunshot, but when it hit me, I fell down. I wasn't even sure where I'd been hit, but something told me to stay down. So I did."

"Was it painful?" I ask.

"I don't remember feeling it then. I was so scared. But then I heard the car door slam. He started the engine and peeled out like he was making a big getaway. Not long after that, I heard another vehicle, which I assumed was the pickup. It wasn't going nearly as fast as Steven, but it wasn't slowing down either. I don't think the driver noticed a thing. I considered standing up and waving, but just like that, the pickup was gone. In the next instant I got up and ran for cover. For all I knew, Steven might be coming back to finish me off. So I ran and ran, finally hiding behind rocks next to some low hills."

"Wow."

"That's when my shoulder and my feet started to hurt. I only stayed long enough to catch my breath. Then I kept going. I had no idea where I was going or why. I suppose I might've been in shock. And although the gunshot wound wasn't serious, blood was everywhere, and for all I knew, I was dying. Even so, I just wanted to get away from Steven."

"I don't blame you."

"Oh, Samantha," says Mom, pointing to the clock, "you're going to be late for school."

"But I—"

"No *buts*. I can finish my story later. You get going."

So without arguing, I grab my stuff and take off. It's a good thing that Olivia and I decided to drive separately today. She has band practice, and I'm going into the precinct. But as I drive to school, all I can think of is my mom...out in the wilderness, bleeding, and frightened. I want to hear the rest of that story!

Fifteen

Before lunch I call Mom just to check on her and make sure she doesn't need me to come home and help her with anything.

"I'm really fine," she assures me. "I'm going to the doctor at three, and after that I'll stop by my office for an hour or so."

"Well, don't overdo it," I warn her.

"Don't worry."

"I'll be at the precinct after school," I say. "But I should be home by five. And I'm fixing dinner tonight."

"Sounds lovely."

"And I want to hear the rest of your story!"

"No problem."

As I close my phone, Olivia walks up. "Everything okay?"

"Yeah, just checking on Mom."

"How's she doing?"

Olivia and I walk to the cafeteria, and I fill her in on Mom's story. Well, the condensed version, but I think Mom would want that. I sense her humiliation for falling for a jerk like Steven and then believing she could get him to come clean. Just the same, I think she was brave to run, and I'm thankful she did.

"And I believe God was watching out for her," I finally say to Olivia. "It's pretty miraculous, really."

"That's incredible," Olivia says.

"But please don't repeat any of the details," I tell her. "I'm not sure Mom's comfortable with it just yet...or ever will be."

"You can trust me, Sam."

"I know."

Conrad and Alex join us for lunch, and I give them an even more condensed version. I can tell they want more details, but they don't push me. I have to appreciate that.

After school I drive downtown, and maybe I'm slightly paranoid, but I go by the park-district building first...just to be sure Mom's car is there. It is. I park nearby, then walk over to the police station.

"Hey, Samantha," says Ebony. She's just coming out of the staff room with a soda. "Want something to drink?"

"I'm good," I tell her.

"Well, come to my office. I have some things to share with you."

Once we're seated in her office with the door closed, she asks how my mom is doing. And with Ebony, I go into all the details, sharing everything Mom told me. I think Ebony deserves that much. She can definitely be trusted, plus she's involved from the law-enforcement end.

"That's an incredible story, Samantha."

"I know. And I haven't even heard the end yet...although I know it ends well."

"Yes, and hopefully the FBI will freeze Greg's funds and your mom will get something back."

"I don't even care about the money. I'm just glad she's safe."

"Absolutely." Ebony reaches for a file folder now. "I've been doing a little research on your friend Brandon."

"And?"

"And you're right. He has been seriously bullied."

"*Has been?* Meaning he's not now?"

"I'm trying to figure that out. I spoke to his mother. She works at the Marriott."

"The Marriott where the proms are held?"

"The same one. Apparently Brandon works there too. Not as a regular, but when they're short-handed, like for a convention or seminar. His mom is divorced and raising him on her own. She said he was identified as gifted when he was young. Back then he was a rather precocious kid and even, according to her, a little full of himself. He would win all the spelling bees and mental math contests, and he started to get picked on in grade school."

"Oh…"

"But she said he figured things out as he got older. He seemed to learn how to avoid conflict, and until last year she thought he was doing okay."

"What happened?"

"She isn't completely sure. But for whatever reason, some of his old classmates began picking on him again. She said he got really beat up a few times, and eventually she complained to the school."

"And?" I feel indignant for Brandon's sake now. How many times does a kid need to get beat up before a school listens?

"She said the administration was understanding and tried to work things out, but finally they recommended a transfer and a fresh start."

"Which is why he's at Fairmont?"

"Right. They actually thought he'd be safer at the rich kids' school. Their thinking was that bullying is less common at affluent schools."

I consider this but wonder. "Is that true?"

"I don't know."

"Did you ask whether he's been bullied at Fairmont?"

"According to his mom, he hasn't been."

"But maybe he doesn't tell her everything. Maybe he doesn't want to worry her."

"Maybe…but she seemed to think everything was fine. She even said that Brandon seemed happier at Fairmont."

"That doesn't make sense though. Why would I be getting those visions?"

"I don't know." Ebony frowns. "Unless it's somehow related to the prom dreams. Do you think that's possible?"

"I don't see how, exactly. I mean, it's interesting that his mom works at the Marriott—and that he does too."

"Yes, I felt the same way."

Now I remember the laundry basket scene. It seemed like a school locker room, but maybe it was part of the hotel—perhaps the laundry room there. "Do you think a bullying incident is going to happen at the hotel and somehow it's related to the prom?"

"I don't know. What do you think?"

"In my last vision he was definitely taking a beating. But the location was hard to figure out. I assumed it was a school, but now I wonder if it could be a laundry room. I wonder if he ever works in the laundry at the Marriott."

"We'll look into it, Samantha."

"And look into the guys he works with. Maybe some are from his old high school. Maybe there's a connection."

"Maybe…" Ebony writes down more notes.

"I just want him to be safe, Ebony," I say. "Before anything worse happens, I want things to change for him."

"Things *are* going to change."

"How?"

"To start with, I'll contact the Fairmont High administration to make sure they have a bullying policy in place. I'll also do some more investigating on Brandon and his work and his friends at school."

"You mean his enemies."

"Yes. I'll see what I can find out."

"And if I can talk to him on Friday when I do my surveillance before prom night, maybe Brandon will reveal something that will explain what's going on and why God keeps giving me these visions."

"Maybe you can get him to open up to you. It's possible that some harassment has already started—something he hasn't told anyone about. Perhaps it's starting to escalate and putting him at serious risk. You need to find out anything and everything you can—and then get in touch with me."

"Yes," I agree. "Brandon may be the only one with those answers."

"I think that's about all we can do at the moment." Ebony smiles now. "Look, Samantha, I want you to do something for me this week, okay?"

"Sure. What?"

"I want you to be a normal girl. Give yourself a couple of free days. Don't come to the precinct. Instead, relax. Hang with your friends."

"Are you sure?"

"I'm positive. You've been through a lot lately. Not just this prom thing but the whole deal with your mom. I want you to have a little break."

"Okay…"

"Thanks."

"Thank you," I tell her.

"And now you can go home…and just have a break."

"Okay." I stand and then pause. "But before I forget, Ebony…"

"Yes?"

"I want to thank you for this weekend. I mean, I don't know what I would've done when Mom was gone…if I hadn't had you to lean on."

She nods. "I was glad to be there for you."

"Mom appreciated you too."

Ebony's face brightens in a big smile. "That's nice to hear."

I stop by the grocery store on my way home. I don't get much, just a few things for a green salad and a loaf of french bread, because I know that will make Mom happy. Then I get home in time to make spaghetti to go with it.

"How nice," Mom says when she gets home and sees the table set and food ready to eat.

"I should probably do this more often," I admit.

"I know you're busy, Samantha. I don't expect this."

Soon we are seated and eating, and I'm waiting for her to continue her story, but instead she talks about her visit to the doctor and work-related things. Finally, as we're finishing, I ask her to tell the rest of the story. "I've been waiting all day," I say.

She nods and sets her napkin on the table. "Right…where did I leave off?"

"You were shot, scared, hiding, afraid Steven might return."

"Well, after a while I could see the sun was going down, so I tried to figure out where I was and where the road was, and I began walking that way. Of course, by then I was well aware that my feet were bare…and not in good shape. Also, I knew I'd lost blood, and the night air was starting to get cool. I thought the best thing might be to try to find a somewhat sheltered place to spend the night and wait for daylight."

"Right."

"So I found a spot next to a big rock that seemed sort of protected, and I settled into it. But then I got even more scared, more upset, and I began to imagine things like rattlesnakes, scorpions, and other wild animals. I thought about cougars or packs of coyotes being able to smell my blood, and I became so frightened that I felt like I was having a heart attack." She pauses and looks at me. "Do you think that's crazy?"

"Not at all. I've read that it's possible for people to be literally scared to death, and I'm sure that was horribly frightening."

"I felt so desperate and scared that I really did begin to pray. And as it got darker and colder, I prayed even harder. I just dumped everything on God. I cried and pleaded, and after a while I felt this amazing presence." She takes a deep breath. "And I believe it was God."

"I'm sure it was."

"And I honestly felt like I met God, almost like face to face, out there in the desert. I know it sounds kind of silly to say it in a safe place and in the light of day, but it was very real, Samantha."

"I have no doubt."

"And I told God that I wanted to give my life to Him. I knew I'd made a mess of it. I wanted Him to do the leading from now on."

"That is so cool, Mom."

She nods. "It really was…and then the strangest thing happened. I probably wouldn't tell this to anyone but you, Samantha, but I felt like your dad was there with me too. It was as if the three of us, God and your dad and me, were all sitting out there in the desert together. Does that sound pretty nutty?"

"No, not at all." Then I tell her how Zach and I have experienced this same thing. "I can't explain it," I say, "but I think maybe God lets Dad check in on us from time to time, especially when we need it."

"Yes…I think so too."

"That is awesome, Mom." I get up and go over and hug her now. "I'm so glad for you."

"I'm not really sure what the next step is for me, Samantha. I mean, I'm still me, and I know I'm still going to make mistakes. But from now on I want God in my life. I don't want to do it alone anymore. I don't think I even can."

"I'm so glad," I tell her. Then I laugh as I begin to clear the table.

"What's so funny?" asks Mom.

"I was just thinking about this promise I made to God when I was all freaked about you being out there."

"What promise?"

"I told God I would never preach at you about being a Christian again. I said that I would accept you as you are."

She laughs too. "Well, I hope you'll still do that."

"Of course. But it looks like God was a few steps ahead of me."

"Ahead of all of us." Mom sets her plate in the sink. "You know, after it was all said and done, after I was safe at the hospital and talking to the FBI people and hearing that Steven had been caught…"

"Yes?"

"Well, I think I was tempted to disregard what had happened out there in the desert. A part of me wanted to chalk it up to desperation and dismiss it as nothing."

"But you didn't."

"No, because when the FBI woman told me about your dream, Samantha—explaining in detail how specific it had been—I got this strange sensation, almost like a jolt of electricity, not like anything I've felt before."

"What was it?"

"I think it was God telling me to pay attention—to credit Him for giving you that dream. And not to sweep it under the rug."

I nod as I rinse a plate. "That sounds about right."

"And I got the same feeling this morning when you mentioned that bit about the vultures and coyotes picking my bones clean. That was exactly what I had thought—verbatim."

"Because God just tuned me in, Mom."

"Because *you were listening,* Samantha."

And I suppose that's true. I *was* listening. But it's easy to listen when it's your own loved one's life at stake. I just pray I can listen that well for others. Even for strangers like the girl in the pale green dress and her friends. And for Brandon. I just hope I'm fully tuned in.

Sixteen

t's fun acting like a normal kid for a few days. I take Ebony's suggestion to heart, and I simply focus on school and friends and life. But by noon on Friday, I know it's time to "go to work" again. Ebony has excused me for a half day, and just as lunch starts, I drive over to Fairmont, where I am given a visitor's pass. I start with the cafeteria, hoping I'll spot someone from my dream. Preferably the girl in the pale green dress.

As I walk across campus, I sense that Fairmont is quite different from Brighton. For one thing, I am immediately aware that this is a very affluent school. Not just by the cars in the parking lot or the way kids are dressed, but by the way they act…and the way they treat me. They don't snub me in a way that's terribly obvious, but it's clear I don't measure up to whatever they measure people by. Mostly I am ignored, as if they are looking right over my head. I begin to feel almost nonexistent.

As I stand in line to get something to eat, I overhear a group of guys talking. I'm sure they don't realize a girl is listening. Or maybe they don't care. But what they're saying totally disgusts me. Apparently these guys have shelled out big bucks for tomorrow night's prom. They have rented their tuxedos, ordered flowers, reserved tables at the most elite restaurants, and even rented a stretch Hummer limo. And now they are counting the hours until the grand finale, because they expect to be paid back for all this—*with sex*. They've already booked rooms at the Marriott, and they're stealing liquor from their parents. And they expect their girlfriends to reward them. One guy actually brags about the fact that his girlfriend is still a virgin. Another guy offers him some nasty suggestions. As I put a chef salad on my tray, they erupt in laughter, and I feel like I want to throw up. All over them.

Instead, I pay for my food and get as far from them as I can. I sit near a table that's filled with some very chatty girls. Maybe even some of those guys' girlfriends. And I can tell by the way these girls talk and act that they consider themselves to be in the highest echelon of Fairmont High society. Whatever. Without looking too obvious, I try to watch and listen, hoping I'll pick up on something or notice someone. As I poke at my salad, which looks totally unappetizing now, I pretend to be reading a book and taking notes. But I'm actually taking notes on their conversation.

"Can you believe those three?" says one girl in an overly loud voice, like she doesn't care who listens or perhaps even wants them to hear her. "Those girls go off and book themselves for the entire day at Oak Springs and don't tell the rest of us so we can get in on it too."

"I wouldn't have gone anyway," says another girl in a flippant tone. "I mean, we're talking about a prom here. It's not like it's your wedding. Get real."

"Still…a whole day of pampering at Oak Springs. Who cares if it's only for a prom?"

"Yeah," says another girl. "I'd do it just for the fun of it. Although my mom would kill me if she found out. Last time I skipped I was in big trouble when I got home."

"Leah's parents don't care," says the first girl. "I know for a fact that they let her do whatever she wants."

"How about Selena's parents?"

"Well, they probably do care."

"I think you're getting way too worked up over it, Chelsea. I mean, get a life, girlfriend."

And then the five-minute bell rings, and the little party breaks up. Still, I think I might have something here. I look at what I've written down. Oak Springs—I'm guessing that's a day spa. I think I've seen ads for it. Leah and Selena and the nameless third girl must be the "it" girls, the ones the others look up to and envy and gossip about. And I suspect that one of those girls has a celadon green gown to wear tomorrow night.

I'm on my way to the counselor's office with my new information when I see Brandon coming around a corner.

"Hey, Brandon," I say, catching him totally off guard.

He squints and adjusts his glasses. "Who are you?"

"Remember last weekend...the arcade?"

"Oh yeah." He comes closer and peers curiously at me. "What's your name again?"

"Samantha."

"So what are you doing here? I thought you went to Brighton."

Without even batting an eyelash, I tell him a flat-out, bald-faced lie. "I just got transferred," I say quietly. Then I glance around as if I'm embarrassed for anyone to overhear this.

"When?" he demands.

"I requested it earlier this week. Today is my first day. Right now I'm heading to the counseling center to set up my schedule with Mrs. Freeman."

"Seriously?" He looks skeptical but interested. "Why are you transferring?"

"You know, it's weird seeing you right now." I shake my head as if trying to take this in. "But I think it hit me when I saw those bullies coming after you at the arcade. Like something in me just snapped—like I cannot take this anymore. Ever since the beginning of the school year, I've been bullied by this gang of girls. For some reason they totally hate my guts. And last weekend I thought, *Why do we take this crud*? I realized I'd had enough. And I thought, *Why not just switch schools*?"

He's looking at me with suspicion now, and I remember this is a really smart kid. I wonder if he can see right through me. "Why Fairmont?" he asks.

"Because my aunt lives in the district," I say casually. "My parents are split up, and my mom's boyfriend is a total psycho. It just seemed like a good escape."

"That *is* really weird." He's softening a little.

"I know. But I think no one will bug me here. It doesn't seem like that kind of school."

He scowls. "Don't be too sure."

"What do you mean? I figured these rich kids would think they were too cool to bother with something like bullying."

"Every school has bullies."

I shrug. "But no one knows me here…well, besides you."

"Well, maybe if you keep it that way."

The tardy bell rings now. "Do you need to go to class?"

"Nah."

"You could do this too, Brandon."

"What?"

"You could transfer out of here to another school…to get away from the bullies."

He sort of laughs now. "I've already tried that."

I act surprised. "Really?"

"Yeah. I transferred from McKinley."

"No way."

He nods. "At first I thought this was better…"

"But it's not?"

He just shakes his head.

"Those kids at the arcade?" I ask. "Were they from here?"

"Yeah."

"They didn't really look like Fairmont types," I point out.

"You're right. They're like the bottom feeders of the school."

I let out a discouraged sigh. "So, was it a waste of time to transfer here?"

Now Brandon actually smiles. "Not as far as I'm concerned. I'm glad you're here."

"Well, thanks," I tell him. Then I feel guilty…because I'm not really here. But maybe I can help him. "Have you ever told?" I ask in a quiet tone. "I mean, when you've been bullied?"

"Not here."

"But at McKinley?"

"Yeah, and that backfired."

I nod. "I know how that goes."

"No place is safe."

"I've heard that some schools have antibullying policies."

"I've never seen one that worked."

I nod. "Yeah, probably not."

"I'd better get going, Samantha. But it was cool talking with you. I'm glad you're here."

"Same back at you." But as I say this, I think I need to somehow straighten this out. But how can I tell him the truth without losing his trust?

One thing at a time, I tell myself as I go to the counseling center. Concern number one is the terrorist threat at the prom. If I can somehow uncover that Fairmont is really the school at risk, we can either have a full-force security team there or perhaps even shut the prom down.

Once I'm in Mrs. Freeman's office, I explain who I am and why I'm here.

"Yes…" She removes her reading glasses and frowns at me. "We've already heard about you."

I can tell by her tone that she's not taking this seriously. I am an aggravation she's being forced to tolerate. "I have a couple of questions in regard to our investigation."

"Yes?"

"I overheard the names of two girls, girls who are absent today—actually there are three, but I only got the names of two. My guess is these are fairly popular girls, and one of them might be a girl that we're specifically concerned about."

"Their names?"

"I only have first names: Leah and Selena."

She nods. "Yes, that would probably be Leah Weis and Selena Moore."

I jot down their last names. "I don't want to get them into trouble, but I think they might be spending the day at Oak Springs."

Her lips twist into what is almost a smile. "Getting a little pre-prom pampering."

"Apparently."

"That's nothing new. We were actually surprised that more girls weren't absent today. It's been a problem in the past. Not that I blame the girls—I'd love a day at Oak Springs myself." She pats her carefully styled platinum hair and sighs. Then she looks back at me. "And now that you know who the girls are, I suppose your work here is done?"

"Not quite."

"Certainly the police don't plan to intervene due to truancy, do they?"

"No, not at all. I just need to see the girls or their photos so we can identify them for future reference."

She stands, goes to her shelf, and removes a yearbook. Then she opens it and flips through until she finds the student section. First she points to a beautiful dark-haired girl. "That's Selena Moore," she tells me.

I nod. "Okay."

Then she flips a few pages, clear to the end and to a page I must've missed. She points to a strikingly pretty blond girl. "That's Leah Weis."

I control myself from jumping up and down. But I know that's her. That's the girl with the pale green dress. This is the right school—the one in my dream! "Thank you," I say calmly.

"Is that all?"

Now I remember Brandon. "No, that's not all," I say. "I'm curious as to whether your school has an antibullying policy."

She laughs. "Are you suggesting we need one?"

"Actually, I am."

She shakes her head. "Look, I know that your little city police department thinks highly of you, dear, and I'm sure you're having a lot of fun skipping school and playing Nancy Drew, but you clearly don't have a clue about our school."

"What do you mean?"

"Fairmont is not the kind of school where bullies and gangs exist. Oh, I'm not saying we don't have our problems. But I think our student body is a bit more sophisticated than what you may be used to over on your side of town."

"So you really don't believe bullying occurs here."

She shakes her head. "No, I do not."

I refrain from rolling my eyes and simply excuse myself. The main thing is that I have the information I need regarding the prom. I can't wait to tell Ebony. The school day's not over, but my work here is done. And to be honest, this place is creeping me out. Okay, I know these rich kids aren't that different from me and my friends. And I just got a sample of something that's probably the worst of the worst. But just the same, they make me sick.

And here's the really sad thing: I think I almost understand why an Islamic terrorist might justify an attack on these kids. Of course, something like that would be wrong and horrible and tragic. But for a split second I almost see American culture in a way that's similar to their twisted perspective, and it scares me. All that immorality, selfishness, and materialistic, self-absorbed godlessness is truly sickening.

I try to shake these thoughts as I get in my car. I know I'm being totally judgmental and critical, and God does not think like that. I take a moment, asking God to clear my head of all this…to give me, once again, His perspective. And then I pray for the students at Fairmont. I pray that they might recognize their shallowness…and see their need for God.

Then I start my car, and as I pause before exiting the parking lot, glancing over at the decorative stone wall in front of the school, I experience that familiar flash of light. But instead of seeing the shiny brass letters that spell out Fairmont High illuminated in the sunlight as it was when I arrived about an hour ago, the sky is now cloudy, and I see bouquets of flowers and wreaths and stuffed animals and enlarged photos and posters and a big black ribbon tied loosely around the whole thing…and some students are standing alone, others are huddled or embracing, but almost everyone is crying.

With cold clarity, I realize that the school sign has been transformed into a memorial of sorts. The students are paying tribute to friends who were slain…shot down in cold blood at their high school prom. That's when I know I will do everything humanly possible to stop this. And I believe that God will do the rest.

am certain," I tell Ebony. "It's Fairmont."

She nods as she finishes her notes, recording what I've just told her, how I've identified Leah Weis as the blonde in the pale green dress and then my vision of the mourners at the school sign. She looks at me, puts down her pen, and sighs. "It's such a huge relief to have it pinned down. But that means our work is about to seriously begin, Samantha. No more playing around."

"Pulling in the forces?"

"Absolutely."

"You don't think they'll want to cancel the prom altogether?" I ask as I remember that last disturbing vision. If it were up to me, I would rather cancel the prom than risk something like that.

"We'll definitely make that recommendation to the school, although I doubt they'll take us too seriously. So far no one else has, and I have to admit it would be great to catch these terrorists red-handed. I know we'd all like to lock them up before they get a chance to strike someplace else."

"I agree."

"The best plan might be to allow the prom to go as planned, but the hotel will be crawling with security."

"Will the FBI be involved now?"

"Yes. Since we have this nailed, I don't know that you need to be part of the action." She picks up her phone. "Excuse me. I have a lot of calls to make."

"So I don't get to work undercover at the prom?"

"How do you feel about it?"

I consider this. "To be honest, I would've been glad to be excused just a couple of hours ago, but now I don't want to miss out."

"What changed your thinking?"

"Mostly that last vision. Before that, I was a little fed up with those Fairmont students...I kind of didn't care."

"And now you do?"

I nod. "Totally."

"Well, it would be great to have more insiders. And you're the one God's been sending the signals to. You never know if there could be another one coming. I'd like to have you around to help."

"I want to be there."

"And we'll have plenty of people watching you, Samantha. We can keep you on the sidelines with us and away from anything dangerous. Trust me, I'll have my eyes on you. Speaking of watching you, why don't you rent a gown in a striking color?"

"Like what?"

Ebony thinks for a moment. "Perhaps magenta or electric blue. Something that will be easy to spot."

"You got it."

I am feeling totally jazzed as I drive away from the police station. I know my high spirits would seem weird to some people…like how can I be excited that a high school prom could be attacked by terrorists? What's wrong with me? But I'm focusing on the fact that I believe not only will this crime be prevented but the perpetrators will be locked up by tomorrow night. I suppose I really am a crime solver at heart. Maybe it was genetic, passed on to me by Dad. Or just a gift from God. Whatever it is, I cannot wait to see this thing put to rest.

When I get home, I tell my mom a little about what's going down tomorrow. At first she reacts like always, uptight and concerned and not really wanting to hear about it. But suddenly she changes.

"Tell me more, Samantha."

"Really? Like details and everything?"

She nods. "Yes—everything."

"And it won't upset you?"

She just smiles. "After all I've been through and how your gift helped rescue me and how it also helped your brother, let's just say that you—and God—have made me a believer."

So I launch into the whole story. She listens intently, and although I can see some of it is unsettling to her, she seems fairly okay with it.

"And Ebony guarantees your safety?"

"Absolutely."

"And you'll be really careful?"

"Of course, Mom. Ebony has trained me in surveillance and that sort of thing. The first rule is to stay out of danger."

"And God will be watching over you."

"As always."

She nods. "Well, then it sounds like it's settled. And this time I'll be praying for you too, Samantha. I feel so bad that until now you've been sort of on your own."

I can't even say how happy this makes me, so I just hug my mom. "Thanks!" Then I realize I might be hurting her shoulder, but she says it's much better.

"In fact, I'm going out tonight."

Okay, now I feel disappointed. Is she going out to the bars with Paula again? Isn't that how this whole mess with Steven (a.k.a. Greg Hampton) began? But I don't say anything.

"I can tell by your face that you're worried," she says.

I shrug. "A little."

She just grins. "Well, don't worry. I'm going out with Ebony. She invited me to the singles group at her church."

"Oh, Mom!" I clap my hands. "That's awesome!"

"I thought you'd like that."

"And I'm going out with Conrad and Olivia and Alex tonight."

"Good for you."

So it is that I have an enjoyable evening being a normal girl, hanging with my friends, acting like I'm just like them. And really, I am. Only different. But then, we're all different.

"Oh yeah," Conrad says as we're having pizza after the movie. "I can't believe I forgot to tell you guys. My mom called from Seattle this afternoon. The first tests are in, and Katie is already responding to the new meds. The doctors are feeling really optimistic."

"That's fantastic," I tell him.

"But we still want everyone to keep praying for her," he reminds us.

"For sure," says Olivia.

As we're sitting there, being happy, normal teens and just living our lives, I think about the Fairmont students I observed yesterday. Okay, I got a little fed up, and it's obvious they have their problems, but even so, they deserve more times like this. And I'd like them to have more time in hope that they might arrive at a place of faith, a place like my friends and I enjoy on a daily basis. And I know I'll be praying for them a lot during the next twenty-four hours.

Olivia, for the third time, accompanies me to the rental shop. By now the woman working there knows us by name. And she must think I'm the most popular girl in the greater Portland area.

"Ebony said something bright," I instruct my fashion consultant Olivia as we dig through the racks. "She suggested magenta or electric blue."

"Whoa, that is bright."

I already told Olivia the details of yesterday's investigation and my latest vision. As always, she promises to be my prayer partner tonight.

"How about this little number?" she suggests as she holds up what looks like a bad bridesmaid dress in a blue so bright it makes my teeth hurt.

"I don't think I want to stick out quite that much," I say.

After several tries we finally settle on a pinkish-purple dress, which the saleslady assures me is magenta. It's really a fairly simple design and fits like a glove, but because the shiny fabric has some stretch in it, I think I should be able to maneuver pretty well.

"Does it look cheap though?" I ask Olivia, the expert.

She narrows her eyes critically. "Not cheap. I mean, it's a little too flashy to be considered elegant. But it has a look that's pretty sophisticated. If you put the right accessories with it—and I think I have something you can use—and if you'd let me pick out the shoes for this one, I think you might pass for a Fairmont chick."

"I don't have much money for shoes," I point out. "Can't I wear the ones I wore last time?"

"No," she insists. "Even if we have to go to Shoes 4 Less, you have to have cool-looking shoes."

When we finally have the outfit together, I have to agree with Olivia: it's not half bad. Then just as we're leaving the mall, my cell phone rings. I pull over to answer it, and Ebony asks me to stop by the station as soon as possible.

"Is something wrong?" asks Olivia as I close my phone.

"I don't think so. Ebony said they're having a meeting regarding tonight."

"Getting their ducks in a row?"

"I guess."

Even so, I feel a little nervous as I drop Olivia at Lava Java to wait for me and I head over to the precinct. I hope nothing's gone wrong. I really hope they're not having second thoughts about me being there tonight. I need to be there. They need me to be there. I'm ready to put up a fight if necessary. And it's a comfort to know that my mom is backing me now. I intend to go!

"Have a seat," says Ebony when I join a small group assembled in the conference room. Eric is there as well as some of the others who have been working the prom stakeouts.

"What's up?"

"Well, we've had some good news," Ebony says.

"What?"

"The terrorists have been caught."

"Caught?" I blink in surprise. "When?"

"Yesterday morning."

"Yesterday morning?" I try to wrap my head around this new piece of information.

"The FBI got a tip from a landlord, and it turned out he was right."

"How many were there?"

"Four."

I nod as I try to absorb this. "Wow…that's great."

"So everyone thinks there's no need to go to the prom tonight."

I nod again, but even as I do this, I feel uneasy.

"What do you think, Samantha?" asks Ebony.

"I'm not sure…"

"I think it's great," Eric says. "I, for one, am about ready to have a free Saturday night." The others echo this sentiment.

"So," says Ebony slowly, "you're okay with this too, Samantha?"

Now it hits me. "Not really," I admit.

"Why?"

"You say the terrorists were picked up yesterday morning, right?"

"Yes. The FBI broke in while they were still asleep."

"But I had that last vision yesterday afternoon, hours after the terrorists were arrested."

"Yes?"

"So why would I get another vision—a very specific vision—if there was no longer any danger?"

"I don't know…" Ebony glances around the group. No one says anything, but I can feel their discomfort as they look away. Like maybe they think I'm confused or possibly getting mixed signals, but they don't want to admit it.

"Is it possible there could be more than four terrorists?"

"I suppose there's always a chance…"

"But the FBI seized all their computers and things," points out Eric. "And they seemed convinced that these four were the main threat in this area."

"Apparently they recently relocated here from Los Angeles," Ebony says. "All four at the same time."

"That may be so," I tell them. "But what if the FBI is wrong? What if there is even one more terrorist? One who is intent on killing high school kids?"

"Then we'd want to be there," Ebony says.

Eric groans.

"Think about it," I say to him. "Would you rather be there and be right…or not be there and be wrong?"

He shrugs. "Obviously I'd rather be there."

"You feel certain about this, Samantha?"

I look around the group, and I know that no one here, maybe not even Ebony, wants to do another prom tonight. I also know I could be wrong. Sometimes my visions and dreams don't come in what I'd consider a chronological order. But am I willing to chance it?

"Here's how I feel," I say to them with conviction. "I plan to go to the prom tonight. And trust me, it's not like I enjoy these stupid functions. Ask Eric if you don't believe me." I glance his way, and he nods to confirm. "But I am not comfortable just stepping away from this thing—not after the vision I had yesterday afternoon *after* the terrorists were safely under arrest. I cannot imagine why God would give me a vision so specific, so horribly sad, if it wasn't still meant as a warning. So whether or not you guys go tonight, I plan to be there even if all I do is stand around the lobby and watch."

"Well, I'm not going to let you do that alone," Ebony says. And slowly, as if their arms are being twisted, the others agree.

"I doubt, however," says Ebony, "that we can talk the FBI into being there now."

"But you will tell them that we're still going?"

"Absolutely," Ebony says. "We will treat this event exactly the same as the others. Whether others want to join us will be up to them."

Still, I feel totally deflated as I head over to Lava Java to meet Olivia. And once again I know that makes no sense. I should be thrilled that the terrorists have been caught. And I am thrilled. But I'm not convinced that the Fairmont students are out of harm's way yet. Yesterday's vision is not something I can simply shrug off.

"What's up?" asks Olivia as I join her.

I quickly give her the lowdown on the arrests of the terrorists and then go up to the counter to order an iced mocha.

"So are you going tonight or not?" she asks when I come back.

"We're going," I say in a downhearted tone.

"But you don't want to go?"

"I do and I don't." I slowly take a sip. "For sure, I don't want to go to another stupid prom. But on the other hand, after that last vision…the memorial…I don't feel like I can skip it either."

She nods. "Makes sense."

I let out a big sigh. "I just don't get it sometimes…"

"What?"

"Why I get stuck with all this crud."

She kind of laughs now. "What do you mean?"

I hold up my hands helplessly. "Think about it, Olivia. Not only crud with people I don't even know but my family too. It's almost like I'm a magnet for trouble."

She really laughs hard now.

"What is so funny?" I demand.

"You."

"Why?"

"Think about it yourself, Sam. God sends trouble your way because He knows you can handle it."

"Handle it?"

"He knows you can do something about it."

"Huh?"

"Because of the gift He's given you. He entrusts you with big things, Sam. Because He knows you can handle them. Your gift helps people. It solves crimes, puts criminals behind bars. What is wrong with that?"

Now I sort of laugh. "I guess you have a point."

"You're just feeling discouraged because tonight's prom isn't all cut-and-dried like you thought it was before. But maybe there's another reason for you to go tonight, Sam. Maybe God has a different plan. Remember what you said about those sleazy guys? Maybe you'll say something that will make them think twice before doing something stupid."

I smile at her. "Yeah, I suppose. Thanks for the encouragement."

And I try to feel encouraged as I drive home, but I still feel like someone took the wind out of my sails. I'll be extremely relieved when this night is over. Even if it turns out that I was all wrong.

Eighteen

Wow," says Mom when I come downstairs dressed for my big night. "Don't you look hot."

"Too hot?" I ask with concern.

She winks slyly. "Well, I just hope that young detective Eric doesn't get any ideas."

"He's got a serious girlfriend." I frown. "In fact, I'm sure he's ticked at me right now for making him give up another night with her."

"But this isn't your fault," she points out.

So I tell her about today's meeting and how the terrorists have been caught. "Everyone was ready to throw in the towel…except me."

"Why's that?"

I remind her of my latest vision. "And that happened *after* the arrests. Why would I see something like that if everything was under control? Do you think God missed a news flash or something?"

Mom laughs. "Not really."

"So I talked them into going tonight, and now I'm feeling kind of guilty…like what if I'm wrong? What if I'm wasting everyone's time again? This will be the third one, and we're all pretty sick of it."

Mom puts her hands on both sides of my face and looks intently into my eyes now. "Samantha, you need to take yourself more seriously. You have a very special, God-given gift. And if God shows you something and you brush it off simply because it looks like it might not be right…well, you will be sorry."

I blink in surprise. "Yeah. You're right."

"Of course I'm right. I'm your mother!" Then she removes her hands from my face and chuckles. "And because I've personally experienced the benefit of your God-given gift, I will never dismiss it again."

"Thanks."

"I think I see your ride out there," she says, nodding toward the front window. "You be careful, Samantha. I'll be praying for you."

"Thanks, Mom."

Then she does something that my mom rarely does. She kisses me on the cheek before she tells me good-bye.

Everyone in the limo is somber tonight. No small talk. No making plans. We all know what we're supposed to do. For a brief moment, I consider apologizing to everyone, but then I remember my mom's conviction. I remember Olivia's encouragement. No, I won't apologize for a God-given gift. If it turns out to be a waste of time again, I will apologize, because that will mean it's my fault. I got it wrong. As we drive to the Marriott, I pray. I beg God to show me if this is a mistake. Then I beg Him to protect my friends in the car as well as the students at the prom. I beg Him to bring this thing to a good conclusion.

Eric doesn't say much as we go into the hotel and to the prom. We're not quite as early as we were for the other two proms, but there's hardly anyone here. I think this must be related to the rich kid thing. They probably think it's ultracool to arrive very late.

"I'm sorry you have to give up another Saturday night," I finally tell him as we're sitting in the lobby, pretending to be absorbed by one another as we sip our punch. "But I'm not sorry that I'm standing by what I believe God showed me."

Eric gives me a little half smile. "Am I acting like a spoiled brat?"

"No…but I do understand. I don't really enjoy this either." Just as I'm saying this, I notice something. "Hey," I tell him, "look who's over there."

Eric glances over to where Brandon is standing at the reception desk again. He's dressed about the same as always, so obviously he's not here for the prom, and he's got his backpack.

"He's probably working tonight." Eric looks back at me.

"Kind of sad, isn't it? I mean, to have to work in the same place where your classmates are partying at their prom?"

He nods. "Yeah. And just in case anyone wants to look into it," Eric says for Ebony's sake, "we have spotted Brandon Allen heading for what we're guessing is work."

"And keep an eye on that laundry room," I add as I remember my vision of Brandon hiding in the towel cart. Ebony already did some investigating of the work situation here, but she said that nothing unusual surfaced in regard to Brandon. According to the manager, all the employees seem to get along just fine.

Then I tell Eric about the high school counselor's attitude toward bullying, and he just shakes his head.

"They're in denial," he says. "Everyone thinks their school is above that sort of thing…or that's the act they put on so that if something does happens, they can pretend they didn't see it coming."

"Too bad." My heart goes out to Brandon as I watch him walking, his head hanging down in a dejected sort of way as he goes through the same side door he used last time. How would it feel to be in his shoes?

Then I tell Eric about my short conversation with Brandon. "I tried to connect with him as someone who's been bullied too."

"Did it work?"

I nod. "Sort of. But he was kind of in denial too. He said there was no point in reporting bullying, that it just makes things worse."

"That might be true in some cases."

"Unless the school adopts a policy. That might change things."

"Hey," says Eric suddenly. "Girl in a pale green dress entering the hotel."

I casually turn around to see that he's right. It is Leah Weis and friends. She looks like she's the belle of the ball as a group of couples walk through the foyer and pause in the lobby. And suddenly it hits me. Tonight's decorations are a little fancier than the previous proms. And someone has strung white lights all around—just like in my original dream. I feel a chill rush through me, and I think this is going to be the real deal tonight.

"You okay?" asks Eric.

"This feels like *the* night." I quickly stand and glance around, trying not to look too suspicious. *"The real deal."*

He stands and takes my elbow in his hand. "So tell me, what's up?"

I quickly explain about the lights and the feeling I just got.

"You got that, people?" he says in a tone that's meant for Ebony and the others. "We're on high alert in here." He looks at me again. "What's next?"

"Let's just stay with that particular group," I suggest, glancing over his shoulder to the couples who've just arrived. "You watch my back, and I'll watch yours."

"You got it."

Trying not to be conspicuous, we sort of meander and follow the group toward the entrance to the prom, casually standing on the sidelines as the couples take turns having photos made. All the while, Eric and I watch everything, and already I can see Ebony and the others at their posts watching intently too. Eventually the group of couples enters the prom, and I can breathe a little more easily for now. For some reason I think they are safer in there. I guess it's because of my original dream—the white lights and marble floor.

"Still feel like this is the big night?" asks Eric with a smile that completely covers the seriousness of this conversation.

"I feel like something is definitely up."

"Let's stay with Leah and her friend," he suggests as the couple steps onto the dance floor. "But not too obviously."

"Sounds good."

So for the next few dances, we keep Leah and her date in our scopes. We now know that Leah's date is Tyler Morris, one of the guys I overheard in the lunch line yesterday. And his friends are the dates of Leah's friends. Of course, this doesn't surprise me. Then the couples take a break from the dance floor and head for the refreshment area. We keep a safe distance and continue to try to be inconspicuous as we follow.

This goes on for nearly an hour, a very long and uneventful hour. Is it possible I'm wrong? Maybe all the terrorists have been arrested and no one is in danger tonight. And yet...something keeps nagging at me. Something—I think it's God—keeps telling me to remain on high alert. *Do not let up. Keep your eyes and ears open. Stay tuned in.*

"Leah and her friends look like they're heading to the ladies' room," I point out as I see them gathering the way girls do as they're about to make a group exit. "I'm going to stay with them."

"Be safe," Eric tells me. Then for the sake of our surveillance buddies, he adds, "While you're in the rest room with the other girls."

I casually stroll across the floor, staying less than twenty feet behind the girls as I follow them into the rest room. A couple of them go into stalls, and the others simply check and touch up their makeup and hair. Feeling conspicuous, I go into a stall, close the door, and just listen.

"Tyler is making such a big deal about getting a room," says a voice that must belong to Leah. "Like he thinks that means I'm going to put out." She laughs.

"They're all acting like a bunch of sex-crazed maniacs tonight," says another girl. "I think we should consider ditching them as soon as the prom ends."

More laughter. Then they discuss hiring a taxi to take them home. But some of the girls aren't so sure. They seem worried that they might lose their boyfriends. "Edmond will freak if I pull a stunt like this," says one girl.

"Let him freak," suggests Leah. "He doesn't own you, Grace."

Then I can hear them leaving. I flush the toilet for effect, and after they're gone, I quickly exit behind them, not letting them out of my sight. I carefully look all around as I walk behind them, but nothing seems to be out of the ordinary. I vaguely wonder about Brandon…and the laundry room. But compared to the danger potential here and now, Brandon's problems seem minor and far away. Something I can deal with later.

As I trail the girls through the lobby, I'm still convinced this is where it will happen—right here in this very lobby. That is, *if* it happens. *If* my dreams and visions were right. And suddenly I hope they're not. I actually hope I'm wrong. Because everything about tonight—the white lights, the marble floor, and particularly Leah, her hair, her dress, even her three diamond earrings—well, it all just seems to add up to the horrible event in my dream. Still, there is no sign of a terrorist or anyone who looks vaguely threatening anywhere.

I feel faintly relieved when the girls go back into the ballroom. I spot Eric, not far from the guys. He smiles as I join him, acting like he's glad to see me, like I'm his date.

"I didn't notice anything out there," I say.

"Did you hear anything from the girls in the rest room? Anything that might clue us in?"

"Just that some of them are having second thoughts about making this an all-nighter." Then I explain how the guys got rooms here. "For the obvious reasons…"

"Here's a word of advice from an older man, Sam. You should always be somewhat suspicious of guys between the ages of seventeen and twenty."

"Is that right?"

He nods. "I know it seems like a gross overgeneralization, but I am convinced that male hormones between those ages are pretty much running amuck."

I laugh as I watch the couples interacting. "Running amuck, you say?"

"That's right. Take it from a guy who remembers."

Now the couples are heading to the dance floor again. Like obedient shadows, Eric and I follow, still keeping a safe distance, although I get the feeling that the couples are beginning to notice us. I catch some curious glances tossed our way, and I can't help but think my overly bright dress is drawing attention, but I try to act completely nonchalant.

"My feet are killing me," I admit to Eric while we're dancing.

"It's those shoes."

"Duh. My friend Olivia picked them out."

"I don't know what it is with women and shoes," he says. "Shelby is the same way. She buys shoes just because they're pretty. And then they ruin her feet. Why don't you just take them off?"

I consider this tempting idea. "But what if I need them?"

He laughs. "For what? You planning on defending yourself with those spike heels? Are you an expert in karate or tae kwon do?"

"No, but that's probably not a bad idea."

"Even so, I think the experts would tell you to lose those particular shoes during a scuffle."

We continue to talk and dance, keeping a vigilant watch on the couples as they work the room. But nothing seems to be happening. And I suppose I am slightly relieved.

As it gets later and I know the dance will soon end, I wonder again if I've been wrong after all. Perhaps all the terrorists really are safely locked up. And shouldn't that make me glad? Everything seems completely quiet and normal here tonight. And with only twenty minutes until the dance is over, it's hard to imagine anything going wrong. And yet I feel uneasy.

"I'm starting to doubt myself," I admit to Eric as we trudge out to the dance floor again.

"It ain't over till it's over."

"Yeah, right."

"And thankfully it'll be over soon."

"Man, do my feet ache. I will be so glad to never go to another prom."

"Not even with your boyfriend?"

"That doesn't seem likely." Then I tell Eric about Conrad being distracted with his little sister and how Olivia and Alex are making plans without us. "I don't really care though. I mean, I'm pretty much prommed out."

"You and me both, sister."

"Hey," I say suddenly. "Looks like Leah and Tyler are getting into a little argument."

"Where are they?"

I give him the clock coordinates that we use to describe locations. "Nine o'clock."

He glances over his left shoulder. "Yeah. I think you're right."

"It looks like she's leaving," I point out. "How about if I follow?"

"I'll stay with Tyler."

So, trying not to look too obvious and trying not to limp, I follow Leah out to the lobby. She walks by where the photos were taken, opens her pretty little silver purse, pulls out her cell phone, and starts to make a call.

I go over to the bench in the center of the lobby now. It's a good place to keep an eye on everything, and acting nonchalant, I pull out my cell phone too. Realizing I cannot stand these shoes for one more second, I slip them off and link their straps over one finger while I hit the speed dial to Ebony.

"I don't know what's up," I tell her, "or if anything's really up. But Leah's in the lobby right now. Eric is with Tyler. And I'm at the bench just keeping an eye on things."

"Stay on the phone," she says in a serious tone. "And keep your distance from Leah, just in case. We have guys spotted around there too."

I try not to glance around and look for them, but this is reassuring.

"Do you think this is *it*?" she asks.

"I don't know."

Just then something catches my eye. And I have to do a double take. It's Brandon, but he's changed his clothes. He now has on what looks like an old-fashioned tux, Western style, long and with tails. First I think maybe it's what he wears to work. Perhaps he's been serving at a Western dinner party. But something doesn't seem quite right. The jacket is far too large, and something seems to be bulging beneath it.

"Brandon is here," I say quickly into the phone.

"Yes, we saw him," Ebony says calmly. "I think he's working tonight."

"I don't think he's work—" I stop myself as Brandon begins walking directly toward me. He's about thirty feet away, but I can see that he has a very determined look in his eye. And suddenly I know what's going down. I get it. *"Brandon is the shooter!"* The words are in my brain, and I hope I said them out loud. But I'm so stunned I don't know for sure.

*Sometimes God *gives* me a flash, and sometimes I *know* something in a flash. It's hard to say which comes first, or maybe they are one and the same. But like a flash, in a fraction of a second, I know exactly what's going on, and in a sick and crazy way, it all adds up.

Brandon—the kid who's been bullied, the kid I've been trying to help, the kid I've been defending and feeling sorry for—is fed up. Bitter and hurt and angry, he isn't going to take it anymore, and now he's out for revenge. A serious payback. And being that he's brilliant, at least on some levels, he doesn't want to settle for a run-of-the-mill, regular school-shooting style of revenge. No, that would be too mundane. He wants to take out the kids who've tormented him—at their prom. That will make headlines. His fifteen minutes of fame and then some. It's payback time!

In that same split second, with the phone still to my ear, I hear a slight commotion behind me. Leah and Tyler are arguing now. And their friends are chiming in; the guys are telling Leah to "just chill," and the girls are telling the guys to "stay out of it." None of them seems to be aware of the threat coming directly their way.

195

"Brandon," I say with the phone still in my hand, attempting a friendly smile and a casual wave—something to distract him, slow him down. And what else can I do? After all, I'm right here, right in the line of fire.

He pauses and looks at me now. There's a flicker of recognition, and for a moment I think he's going to stop and talk to me. But then he gets a look on his face that chills me throughout as he unbuttons his coat to reveal what looks like an automatic weapon folded in two. His expression is one of cold, hard hatred as he straightens out the gun in one swift motion like this is something he has practiced again and again. And I know, thanks to my training, that I need to get out of the way. Now!

"He's got a gun," I whisper into the phone as I run barefoot from the lobby toward the front entrance. Hovering in the foyer, I hide behind a marble column. *"Brandon is the shooter!"* I say, but I can hear nothing on the other end. I don't know if Ebony is even there, or maybe my phone is dead. Does anyone know what's going on? There is nothing else I can do right now. I must simply follow my orders, obey my training, and stay out of harm's way. So I remain behind the column, and I pray! I pray and pray and pray.

But just as I'm begging God to stop this madness, I hear voices yelling, and then several shots ring out…followed by screams and more screams. And the horrible scene from my dream flashes through my mind again. Blood-splattered prom dresses, kids splayed across the white marble floor, bleeding. Sobbing…death…Monday's memorial at Fairmont High. It's too late.

I cling to the column as tears fill my eyes. I haven't been able to stop this. It's too late… *Oh, God, why?*

"Samantha," says Ebony as she puts an arm around my shoulders, "it's over."

"It's over?" I ask, wiping my face and looking at her.

"They shot him."

"Shot who?"

"Brandon. He pulled out an AR-15 and was about to shoot into the crowd. They had to stop him."

"Is he…is he dead?"

"I think so."

Now I'm really sobbing. Ebony takes me into her arms, and I can tell she is crying too. "I'm so sorry, Samantha. When lives are in danger like that, cops are trained to protect them. That means they shoot to kill… You know that, don't you?"

I nod but continue to cry. Finally I stop and step away, wiping my wet face with my hands. I can hear sirens now. "Did Brandon shoot anyone?"

"No, but his finger was on the trigger."

By the time we get to the scene, someone has already laid a tablecloth over what I know is Brandon's lifeless body. The students, still dressed in their finery, look on with shocked expressions, talking among themselves, saying how close it was, how they could've been dead, how unbelievable this was.

The girls seem more horrified than the guys as they cling to each other and discuss what almost happened. Meanwhile some of the officers, including Eric, are taking names, getting information from the witnesses.

"Come on, Leah," Tyler says finally. He's the first one to make a move to leave as he tugs at her arm. "Let's get out of here."

The other guys are doing the same with their girls, saying, "It's time to leave." Like they're too cool to stick around and watch this anymore. Acting like the party's over and they want to go start another one. And slowly the popular crowd, the A-list couples, begin to trickle away.

I watch with a sense of confused outrage and indignation. I mean, it's not like I wanted to see them dead instead of Brandon. But in a way it seems they should bear some of the blame here. Yet they simply walk away, off to pursue their next pleasure, whatever it might be. It makes me feel sick to my stomach. Brandon is dead…and they're walking away like it's *no big deal.*

My phone is ringing, and it's my mom. She's seen a news flash, which isn't surprising since the media has begun to arrive. They're interviewing the prom kids who stayed behind, as well as some of the police force. I reassure Mom that I'm okay. That only the shooter was killed.

"Oh, that's good."

"Yeah…" I will explain it to her more fully when I get home.

"Let's get you out of here," Ebony says as the press starts getting pushy. "No need to blow your cover."

As she ushers me off, I see a middle-aged woman rushing into the lobby with several others by her side. She's wearing a maid's uniform, and she is sobbing with her arms outstretched in front of her. She collapses to her knees, tearing off the table-cloth to reveal Brandon's face. She falls onto him and makes a sound that reminds me of a wounded animal.

I shudder, and Ebony keeps walking me toward the foyer and then out the door to the limo, now waiting off to one side. There are police cars and emergency vehicles clustered around, stopping traffic from all directions. So Ebony and I simply sit in the back of the unmoving car.

"You were right," Ebony says to me, as if that's a comfort.

"But I didn't figure out that it was Brandon," I say.

"Yes, you did."

"Not in time to save him."

She sighs. "I don't know if anyone could have saved him, Samantha. Even when he saw our undercover cops with guns, he didn't hesitate."

Somehow I can imagine that. I'd never seen such a determined look in my life. Like he wanted to do this or die trying.

"Eric said that Brandon's AR-15 was fully loaded. That means thirty rounds, and he had two more banana clips, each with thirty more, all ready to go. He had ninety rounds of ammo on him, Samantha."

A chill runs down my spine as I consider this.

"Do you know what would've happened if we hadn't gone tonight?"

I slowly nod.

"My theory is that Brandon, with access to a back door, could slip past security, but besides that, he might've had an employee locker to stash these things in. This was a well-thought-out, calculated plan on his part."

"But the bullying—" My voice breaks with emotion. "If Brandon hadn't been picked on, he wouldn't have done this."

"Probably not."

"And those kids." I start to cry again. "They just walked away, Ebony, like it was no biggie. Like they hadn't picked on him, like they hadn't teased him or made his life miserable. Like this had nothing to do with them. And he was lying right there—dead." I put my face in my hands and let the tears fall freely now.

Ebony just lets me cry. She hands me a tissue and waits until I'm done. I appreciate that.

"In a strange way it must be how God feels sometimes," she finally says.

"What?" I look up at her and try to figure this out.

"Oh, I'm not suggesting that Brandon was like Jesus. But how do you think God must've felt when His Son was killed and people just walked away like no biggie? How it must break His heart when people everywhere, including us before we believed in Him and those selfish kids tonight, just continue on their merry ways—totally oblivious to the reason that Jesus died, totally unconcerned that the Son of God was beaten and murdered so mankind could be saved. And yet mankind didn't care."

I nod, taking this in. "I see what you mean."

"Not that I'm saying Brandon is a hero. He most definitely is not. Still, this is a tragedy. And you're right, Samantha, it seems wrong for those kids to simply walk away, taking no blame."

"I wish there was a way to let them—I mean Leah and Tyler and the others—know why Brandon did this. Bullies need to see the consequences. They need to be called to some kind of accountability."

"And schools need to adopt antibullying policies."

"Yes," I say with conviction. "Is there a way to use this—Brandon's death—to force schools to wake up and pay attention?"

"I think we can do that."

"Like the press in there right now. If I wasn't trying to keep a low profile, I'd go in and make a statement."

"How about if I go do that?"

"Would you?"

She nods, and I want to hug her, but instead I say, "Hurry, Ebony! Go and do it while you have their attention. Do it now!"

"I'm on my way," she says as she reaches for the door.

"And I'm praying."

Twenty

For the next few days, the averted prom massacre is the hot topic on the news. Not just locally, but nationally as well. By midweek Ebony and Brandon's mother, whom Ebony has befriended, are even flown out to New York for appearances on several national news shows. Ebony invited me to come along with them, but I told her I'd rather not. I like being able to work with the police and the FBI without the whole world knowing my identity.

Just the fact that people across the country are hearing more about the sobering consequences of bullying—that it leads not only to crime, which is rather rare, but to suicide, which is not so rare—is encouraging. And I'd really like to think that Brandon's death will serve some purpose. I still feel horrible about his death, and I keep asking myself, and God, if there was something more I could have done. Ebony has pointed out that it's similar to the way it went with Felicity; I can offer warnings and advice, but I cannot control people's choices. It reminds me of how God must feel. But then again, I am not God.

"You need to let it go," Olivia says as we walk to the parking lot together after school. I realize that she's been tolerating my unusual quietness these past few days, but she's probably fed up.

"Huh?" I try to play stupid, like I don't have the foggiest idea what she's talking about. Mostly I just want to get in my car and drive home.

"I know you're still feeling bad."

"Of course I feel bad." I turn and frown at her. "Why shouldn't I?"

"It's okay to feel sad about Brandon's death," she says slowly. She's choosing her words carefully, like she doesn't want to offend me. "But it's not okay to keep blaming yourself."

Leave it to Olivia to see right through me. I don't even try to deny this accusation. But I don't respond either.

"I know that's what you're doing, Sam."

I nod now, swallowing against the hard lump that's growing in my throat.

"It's not your fault that Brandon died."

"It sort of is…," I say in a voice that sounds very small and far away even to my ears.

"How is that?"

I consider this. "I should've put two and two together."

"What two and two?"

"God was giving me visions…you know, about the school shooting…and visions about Brandon…at the same time. I should've figured out they were linked."

"And what about Steven or Greg or whoever he is?"

"What about him?"

"Should you have considered that he was somehow linked to that whole thing too?"

"Well, no…"

"And think about what a huge distraction that was to you at the time. No wonder you couldn't put two and two together. You were freaking over your mom, Sam. You were trying to help her—and you *did* help her. Frankly, I'm surprised you could pull it together well enough to make it to the Fairmont prom and figure that whole thing out in time to avoid a huge tragedy."

"But Brandon is still dead."

She nods sadly as she places a hand on my shoulder. "Yes, that's true. But it's not your fault."

"Still…" I feel tears burning in my eyes now.

"Look, Sam," she says in a firm but kind tone, "you are not God."

I glance at her and almost laugh. "Duh."

"And sure, He uses you to help people, but He doesn't plan for you to save the world. Don't forget that's what He sent His Son to do. Right?"

I nod.

"And good grief," she continues. "You're only seventeen, and you're already solving some pretty incredible cases, but I'm sure you have a thing or two yet to learn about detective work."

"That's for certain."

"So don't be so hard on yourself, okay?" Then she hugs me.

"Thanks," I tell her as I step back and wipe my wet cheeks, "I needed that."

"Just remember, you're not Supergirl. You can't save everyone."

"I know."

"But you are pretty amazing."

Even so, I try to patch together the various puzzle pieces of Brandon's case. I just can't quite set this thing aside yet. I want to figure out who the bullies were and why they were bullying him. I figure there is something to be learned here—for everyone. Then, while in New York, Brandon's mother gives Ebony the names of a couple of her son's "acquaintances."

"Why don't you look into it?" Ebony suggests when she calls me Wednesday evening. And so I do.

One of the names on the list—a boy named Aaron who has also been bullied—actually agrees to talk to me. But only if I keep his name strictly off the record.

"No way do I want to get mixed up in any more of this," he tells me as we meet at Lava Java on Thursday after school. "I already have to look over my shoulder as it is."

"Your anonymity will be protected," I promise.

He glances nervously around the crowded coffeehouse, as if he thinks we're being watched. So I remind him that Fairmont High is going to adopt a bullying policy. "Things are going to change," I say.

"Words are cheap," he shoots back at me.

"Trust me, okay?"

He sort of nods. "What do you want to know?"

"Why do you think Brandon was such a victim of bullying?"

"He sort of asked for it."

"How's that?"

"Well…Brandon made extra money by selling papers…"

"Papers?" I frown at him as I try to imagine Brandon being a paperboy.

"You know, like term papers or essays or answers to upcoming tests—that kind of thing."

"Oh…" I nod as it sinks in. Brandon was helping kids cheat.

"He was real smart. I mean, like genius kind of smart. And he was also kind of poor. So he decided to make some money off the guys who weren't as smart he was but who had money."

"By selling them papers?"

"Yeah. And he did make some money, and he actually thought he was going to be making some friends too." Aaron laughs in a humorless way.

"You mean with the kids he sold papers to?"

"Yeah. Brandon was smart in some ways, like academics, but he wasn't too smart when it came to social stuff."

"How's that?"

"He didn't get it. Guys like us are never accepted with the cool kids. We're always on the outside—that's just how it is." He scowls at me now. "Like no way would you be talking to some-one like me if you weren't trying to get something from me."

"That's not true. I have friends from all walks of life, and I—"

"Yeah, whatever." He rolls his eyes.

"Fine," I say. "You don't have to believe me. Just tell me about Brandon, okay?"

"So anyway, he was pretty surprised when some of the jock dudes still picked on him—even after he sold them papers. Nothing really physical or anything, since I think they actually appreciated his academic help. But they'd still tease him. Like if we were in the locker room, you know, guys would say stuff and put us down. You know the kind of crud I mean?"

"Yeah, girls sort of do the same thing sometimes."

"So Brandon decided to get back at them."

"You mean with the shooting?"

"No, it was way before that. He got back at them a couple of months ago."

"What did he do?"

"He gave Tyler Morris an essay that was totally bogus. As a result, Tyler got an F, and because of the failing grade, he was suspended from a pretty critical basketball game during the state play-offs."

"Really?"

"Before that, Fairmont thought they'd win state for sure."

"But they came in third instead?"

"Yep."

"And so Tyler was mad?"

"Not just Tyler. All the jocks were mad. The whole school was mad."

"So the jocks started beating him up?"

"No way. They might get into big trouble for doing some-thing like that. Baseball season was just around the corner, and Tyler is even better at baseball than basketball."

"So what then?"

"They hired hit men."

"Hit men?"

"Basically they were just some thugs that go to our school—the kinds of kids who don't care if they get in trouble, especially if there's a payoff. Naturally, there was."

I remember the guys at the video arcade now. "I'm starting to get it…"

"So for the past several weeks, Brandon was always running and hiding and getting beat up—I mean, seriously beat up."

"But his mom denied this."

"Of course. Brandon was scared. The hit men told him that they'd really make him suffer if he told on them."

"So he kept his mouth shut."

"Yeah. And according to Brandon, they tried not to hit his face too much when they beat him up. But he still had bruises and stuff."

"That's so sad."

"But Brandon was asking for it."

I frown, trying to think of a response. "Still..."

We talk awhile longer, and I try to encourage Aaron to speak to the authorities if anyone picks on him. He acts like it's futile, but I tell him that the only way things will change is if people speak out.

"Part of the bullying policy will be to have some anony-mous ways to report on bullying. You can turn kids in without revealing your identity."

He considers this.

"Just don't let what happened to Brandon happen to you," I say as we finish up. He assures me that it's not even a possi-bility. Then I thank him, and we go our separate ways.

By the end of the week, life seems to have quieted down some. Ebony is back home, and I am feeling more like a "nor-mal girl" (whatever that is) again. I'm also taking Olivia's advice to heart and accepting that I'm not Supergirl—not that I ever thought I was. And I'm making progress about not blaming myself for Brandon's death.

Besides that, we also hear some really good news about Conrad's little sister. It sounds like Katie is doing really well.

Conrad explains that the treatments are complete now, and if her white-cell count continues to improve, she may be completely out of the woods soon.

"In fact, it might not be lupus at all," he explains to us during lunch on Friday. "And they've ruled out almost everything else that's life threatening. The doctors admit they're surprised that this new treatment worked so fast, and my mom keeps trying to tell them that God intervened with a miracle." He laughs. "But medical professionals don't always get miracles. They think it's the new medicine."

"Maybe it's both," suggests Alex.

"Or maybe it's a miracle," claims Olivia.

"Think about it," I add. "Literally hundreds of people have been praying for little Katie—it could be a miracle."

"Anyway, I'm feeling pretty relieved," he says with a happy sigh.

I'm feeling relieved too. Life seems to be settling down now. And I, for one, am ready for it.

Twenty-one

L ater Friday afternoon Conrad walks me to the parking lot where Olivia is waiting to give me a ride home. Just as we're about to say good-bye, he invites me to go to Saturday night youth group with him.

"Yeah," I tell him happily as Olivia comes over to join us. It's a huge relief not to have to make up any excuses this weekend.

"Cool," he says. "I was actually starting to get a little worried."

"Worried?"

"Well, the last time I asked you to go with me to youth group, you gave me some lame-sounding excuse, which I tried to overlook. But when I heard that both you and Olivia didn't go to youth group the weekend Alex and I went to Seattle, I had to wonder what was up."

"Hey, I had an excuse," says Olivia, winking at me. "The Stewed Oysters had a gig that night."

"Yeah, but what was Sam doing?"

I give him a mysterious grin but don't attempt to explain.

"See," he says as if I just proved his point. "And then you wouldn't go to youth group with me again last week."

"I was busy…"

"So you say, but I started to think maybe something was going on with you spiritually…like maybe you were falling away from the Lord."

I have to chuckle at that. "No, silly, I am most certainly *not* falling away from the Lord. I couldn't survive one single day without the Lord."

"And seven days without the Lord makes one weak," he teases.

I punch him in the arm now. "And that joke is as old as the hills and twice as dusty."

"Thanks." He rubs his arm, frowning like he's hurt.

"And thanks for assuming I was falling away from God," I shoot back at him.

"Well, I didn't actually believe that…but you have to admit it was a little puzzling…I mean the way you kept making excuses and stuff."

"Sam just happens to be a woman of mystery," says Olivia with a twinkle in her eye. "But I can attest that she hasn't been up to anything bad."

He nods, then looks slightly uncomfortable as he clears his throat. "No offense, Olivia, but do you mind if Sam and I have a private conversation for a few minutes?"

Olivia pretends to be offended, then just laughs as she walks away. "Fine, I'll be in my car, Sam. If you still want a ride, that is."

"Yeah, she'll need a ride," he calls out. "I promised to run Alex over to the track meet at McKinley, and I'm already late.

"Okay," he says as soon as Olivia is gone. He looks directly at me now, like maybe this is serious, and suddenly I

wonder if he's about to tell me that he wants to date someone else.

"*Okay?*" I brace myself and wait for him to begin.

"Okay…since I'm somewhat assured that your not going to
youth group isn't related to your relationship with God…" He
pauses with an uncertain frown. "What about me?"

"Huh?"

"I figure it could be one of two things. Like maybe you
don't like going to youth group with me. Or maybe you just
plain don't like me."

I throw back my head and laugh now. "No way," I tell him.
"Wrong on both counts."

He grins in relief. "Okay then."

"Okay then."

"So, if you still like me and God both…I have another
question, Sam."

"What?"

"Well, I know it's late notice, especially since it's only a
week away…"

Uh-oh, I think I know where this is heading, and I'm not so
sure I want to go there. Just the same, I keep my mouth shut.

He takes my hand in his now, almost as if he's making a
marriage proposal, which is totally ridiculous. "Samantha McGregor, will you do me the honor of going to the prom with me?"

I'm sure a shadow washes across my face when I hear
that dreaded four-letter *p* word again. Another prom? Just
shoot me. Okay, maybe not.

"You don't want to?" He looks stunned now. As well as a
little hurt.

"No no," I say quickly, regretting my initial reaction. "I'm just totally surprised by this, Conrad. Are you serious?"

"Of course I'm serious. You want to go?"

I smile at him. "I would love to go to the prom with you!"

"Really?"

"Absolutely."

Then he leans down and gives me a quick peck. "Cool."

I nod. "Yeah, cool."

"Well, I gotta go. See ya!" Then he gives this funny little leap for joy before he takes off running to the other side of the parking lot. Who would've thought? A guy who actually *wants* to go to the prom.

I slowly walk over to Olivia's car and try to work up some enthusiasm about another night at a prom.

"What's wrong?" asks Olivia with concern.

"Wrong?"

"You look totally bummed. Did you and Conrad break up or something?"

"No," I tell her.

"What then?" she demands.

"He asked me to the prom."

Of course, this just makes her shriek with joy. "Woo-hoo!" she shouts. "We're going prom dress shopping, girlfriend!"

I nod in resignation. "I can't wait."

She just laughs. "Get over it, Sam."

I do get over it. When the night for the Brighton prom arrives, which is thankfully not at the Marriott, I am totally jazzed. This time I'm not wearing a rental dress or even cheap shoes, not that I would have minded so much, but Olivia held me to my promise. And she helped me find the perfect gown in a pale shade of pink. She also loaned me her pearls again. And my mom got me this pretty little beaded bag that's absolutely perfect. The shoes were a compromise. Because it's a long dress, Olivia said it would be okay to wear a lower heel. But she insisted on picking out a cool style, and I have to admit they're really pretty. Plus, they're also fairly comfortable. No more "killer" shoes for this girl.

"Smile," Mom says as she snaps a photo of Conrad handing me a nosegay of pink rosebuds in the entryway. Then she makes all four of us pose by the fireplace for several more shots. And then another one with me pinning Conrad's boutonniere onto his lapel. The four of us laugh and joke as we partake in the hors d'oeuvres and sparkling apple cider that Mom provided for us. It was so sweet of her to go to that extra effort. And really, she seems happier than she's been in a long time. Even happier than she was with Steven, which, looking back, she admits was a shallow kind of happiness. In fact, she seems happier than she's been since before Dad died. She and Ebony are actually becoming friends now. And they're going to another singles thing at Ebony's church tonight.

"Powder room," says Olivia just before we're ready to leave—not via a fancy limo this time but simply in Alex's parents' roomy sedan.

And as my best friend and I are standing in front of the bathroom mirror, I realize that tonight is totally different from the other three prom nights. Those weren't anything like this. *This is fun.*

"Are you okay?" she asks suddenly.

I give her a serious, wide-eyed expression. "I just had a flash," I say dramatically.

Her eyes look frightened. "Oh no, Sam. Please tell me it's not another shooting."

I laugh loudly. "No, I just had a flash that tonight is going to be fun!"

"Thank God!" she says in relief.

"Yeah," I tell her, "you can say that again!"

And I do thank God as Alex drives us to a restaurant (not the fanciest, most expensive one in town). I thank God, not just for tonight, which I know is going to be totally awesome, but I also thank Him for each and every part of my somewhat complicated life and for the way it never seems to go in a perfectly straight line. Somehow I know, and I firmly believe, that God really is working all these things together for good. Even when it seems really bad, or horribly sad, or totally hopeless, or just plain frightening, I know that if I trust Him—if I hold on tight—He always, always sees me through. And I am thankful!

Reader's Guide

1. Early in the story, Sam is trying to accept her mom's boyfriend. Why do you think this is so hard for her? How did you feel about him?

2. How did you react to Sam's visions in regard to the bullying incidents? Did it make you uncomfortable?

3. How would you feel if you witnessed bullying behavior? Would you get involved? If so, what would you do?

4. Have you ever been the victim of bullying? Or maybe you've been a bully? If so, explain how that made you feel.

5. Sam and her mother seem to be speaking two different languages sometimes. Why do you think communication between them is so difficult? Can you relate to that in your own life? How?

6. Beth's opinions on her daughter's gifts change drastically after Sam's vision leads to her rescue. Do you ever wish something miraculous like that would happen in your own family's relationships? Describe an "everyday" miracle you'd like to see in your own life.

7. Did you suspect that Brandon would be involved in the prom shooting? Why or why not?

8. What did you think of the people whose lives were in danger at the prom? What did you think about their relationship with the shooter?

9. How did you feel when Brandon was the only person shot?

10. Can you imagine what it would feel like to have a gift like Sam's? Do you think it would be a blessing or a curse? Why?

11. What kind of gifts do you have? Explain how you feel about them.

SO YOU WANT TO LEARN MORE
ABOUT VISIONS AND DREAMS?

As Christians, we all have the Holy Spirit within us, and God speaks through His Spirit to guide us in our walk with Him. Most often, He speaks through our circumstances, changing our desires, giving us insight into Scripture, bringing the right words to say when speaking, or having another Christian speak words we need to hear. Yet God, in His sovereignty, may still choose to speak to us in a supernatural way, such as visions and dreams.

Our dreams, if they are truly of the Lord, should clearly line up with the Word and thus correctly reveal His character. We must always be very careful to test the words, interpretations of circumstances, dreams, visions, and advice that we receive. Satan wants to deceive us, and he has deceived many Christians into thinking that God is speaking when He is not. So how do we know if it's actually God's voice we are hearing?

First we have to look at the Bible and see how and what He has said in the past, asking the question, *Does what I'm hearing line up with who God shows Himself to be and the way He works in Scripture?* Below is a list of references to dreams and visions in Scripture that will help you see what God has said about these gifts:

- Genesis is full of dreams and visions! Check out some key chapters: 15, 20, 28, 31, 37, 40, 41
- Deuteronomy 13:1–5
- Judges 7

- 1 Kings 3
- Jeremiah 23
- Several passages in the book of Daniel
- Joel 2
- The book of Ezekiel has a lot of visions
- There are a lot of dreams in the book of Matthew, specifically in chapters 1 and 2
- Acts 9, 10, 16, 18
- The whole book of Revelation

If you want to learn more and have a balanced perspective on all this stuff, you'll probably want to research the broader category of spiritual gifts. Every Christian has at least one spiritual gift, and they are important to learn about. Here is a list of books and Web sites that will help:

- *Hearing God's Voice* by Henry and Richard Blackaby
- *What's So Spiritual about Your Gifts?* by Henry and Mel Blackaby
- *Showing the Spirit* by D. A. Carson
- *The Gift of Prophecy in the New Testament and Today* by Wayne Grudem
- *Are Miraculous Gifts for Today?* edited by Wayne Grudem
- *Keep in Step with the Spirit* by J. I. Packer
- www.expository.org/spiritualgifts.htm
- www.desiringgod.org. Click on Resource Library and choose Topic Index. Then under Church & Ministry, check out Spiritual Gifts under Church Life.

(Note: If you're doing a Google search on spiritual gifts or dreams and visions, please make sure you type in *Chris-*

tian as well. This will help you weed out a lot of deceitful stuff.)

As you continue to research and learn about spiritual gifts, always remember: the bottom line is to focus on the Giver, not the gift. God gives to us so we can glorify Him.

> Signs and wonders are not the saving word of grace; they are God's secondary testimony to the word of his grace. Signs and wonders do not save. They are not the power of God unto salvation. They do not transform the heart—any more than music or art or drama that accompany the gospel. Signs and wonders can be imitated by Satan (2 Thessalonians 2:9; Matthew 24:24), but the gospel is utterly contrary to his nature. What changes the heart and saves the soul is the self-authenticating glory of Christ seen in the message of the gospel (2 Corinthians 3:18–4:6).
>
> But even if signs and wonders can't save the soul, they can, if God pleases, shatter the shell of disinterest; they can shatter the shell of cynicism; they can shatter the shell of false religion. Like every other good witness to the word of grace, they can help the fallen heart to fix its gaze on the gospel where the soul-saving, self-authenticating glory of the Lord shines. Therefore the early church longed for God to stretch forth his hand to heal, and that signs and wonders be done in the name of Jesus.
>
> —John Piper, *Desiring God*

About the Author

MELODY CARLSON is the award-winning author or more than one hundred books for adults, children, and teens. She is the mother of two grown sons and lives near the Cascade Mountains in central Oregon with her husband and a chocolate Lab retriever. She is a full-time writer and an avid gardener, biker, skier, and hiker.

Faced with her son's crystal meth addiction and her husband's affair, Glennis Harmon searches for the ways she can best reach and help those she deeply loves.

Real-life struggles. A family's pain.
A hope for healing.

Bright and ambitious, college student Alice Laxton is diagnosed with schizophrenia—and embarks on a painful and eye-opening journey toward recovery and healing.

Diary of a Teenage Girl series
Meet Chloe

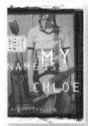

My Name is Chloe

Join Chloe at the beginning of a wild ride to stardom in the Christian music industry—a place where life is unpredictable and only God knows what kind of twists and turns wait on the road ahead.

Sold Out

Former social outcasts Chloe, Allie, and Laura are stoked when their band Redemption sky-rockets to contemporary Christian pop stardom. But the girls find out fast that fame comes with a price tag. Can the band—or their friendship—survive this?

Road Trip

Chloe, Allie, and Laura set off on tour as the opening act for the most popular Christian band in the country, Iron Cross. Still, life on the road gets less and less glamorous and more and more over-whelming—especially when Laura begins acting strangely. Her hostility toward Chloe's concern makes the girls wonder how much longer they can keep their act together.

Face the Music

Amid a grueling con-cert schedule, Chloe realizes that her attraction for the lead singer of Iron Cross is a powerful and even dangerous force. But when death hits close to home, Chloe is slammed by another emotion: guilt. Learn with Chloe that there comes a time when we all have to face the music.

Now available in bookstores and from online retailers.
www.doatg.com

Diary of a Teenage Girl series
Look inside
Kim's life

Just Ask

On her quest to get a car, Kim begins to write the anonymous teen advice column for her dad's newspaper. Most letters deal with everyday problems...nothing that Kim can't handle. But when a classmate is killed, the letters turn to questions about life, death and what it all means, Kim starts to wonder where to find the answers. Who can she turn to—just to ask?

Meant to Be

Kim's mom has stage four ovarian cancer, and Kim knows that the odds are dismal. Her mom makes her promise that she'll continue with life as normal. But how can life be normal with cancer hanging over your head like a dark cloud?

Falling Up

How much stress can a girl take? When Kim reaches the breaking point, her dad sends her off to her grandmother's house in small-town Florida where she's able to slow down and instead of falling apart, she can fall up...into His arms.

That Was Then

Kim's best friend, Nat, is pregnant and soon to be married to Ben O'Conner, Caitlin's younger brother.

Nat is starry-eyed, believing that once she and Ben are married, God will bless them because they are doing the right thing. Kim is not so sure—is marriage the only solution for two seventeen-year-olds with a baby on the way?

CPSIA information can be obtained
at www.ICGtesting.com
Printed in the USA
LVHW031127240521
688317LV00001B/142

9 781590 529348